Romance, Runaways and

Rock n' Roll

A Nikki Rodriguez Mystery

M.A. Hansen

I0556879

This book is a work of fiction. The characters, incidents, story, and dialog are drawn from the author's imagination. None of the characters are real. Any resemblance to actual events or living or dead persons is entirely coincidental.

Cover art is designed by Mariah Sinclair, <u>mariahsinclair.com</u>

Prologue

"The building of the new youth center is perfect!

A two-story building on two acres of land, complete with a tennis

court, a basketball gym, a baseball diamond, a sandy volleyball

court, a small outdoor track, and a small football field. It was once

a private school that was renovated from an old winery. This

building needs moderate repairs and some light renovations. Easy

stuff that can be completed in three weeks." Nikki said as she led

the group through the grounds of the Youth Center. She then

brought them into the Spanish-style building from the 1920s.

Donors and select city departments and guests had a first view of

what this marvelous place would become.

Nikki guided the tour with Paul right by her side. The day began

with a groundbreaking, and Nikki said a few words. Next came the

tour and to end it all some refreshments in the gym would be

served. The visitors today were very pleased with the plans in

motion to bring this all to light. Nikki received many

congratulations and kind words of appreciation.

Nikki knew this would be a big benefit for the youth of her community. She was very happy and brimming with pride in her soft pink pants suit. Paul was inspired by Nikki; he smiled at her for her generosity and her drive to give and support so many. Unselfishly, she gave to everyone. He thought the world of her, and he loved her...

The mayor turned toward her to say, "Nikki, you have outdone yourself, bravo! I have had so many calls to my office about the youth center. We have calls from volunteers, teachers, and tradespeople wanting to donate supplies and classes.

We have been so busy, and I would like to add that our Senator from California has contacted me for all of the details of the youth center. It seems that Rancho Niguel is catching the eye of Washington DC." Mayor CJ Groves was still giddy and cuddly with Nikki ever since her stepfather, Jeff, made the mayor's wishes come true. No doubt she would use this for her political gain, but for Nikki, she was just happy to give this to the youth of her community.

Paul looked like he knew exactly who the mayor was, his psych degree analyzing her. He didn't like her, but he tolerated her and, of course, Stacie Mc. Daniel's was a buffer for the mayor.

Before Nikki could steal Paul away from the mayor, Stacie

intercepted and led Paul to get a drink at the makeshift bar set up

on the other side of the gym.

Stacie smiled and made sure Nikki's eyes were on them. Nikki knew

a few weeks ago her suspicion was correct. Stacie wanted Paul

back.

Chapter 1

Sara Ran Away

"I'll stand by you." I ended the song by The Pretenders. We finished the music lineup for Kendle's annual Valentine's Day Dinner. "That sounds good, Nikki, but I think we should add a few more rock ballads, love songs, you know, like, "Every Rose Has It's Thorn" and maybe something by KISS and Red Hot Chili Peppers, that would be cool," Roxy said.

"Ok, ladies, let's add a few more rock n' roll love songs."

After practice in my garage was over, the band went home, and I walked back to my condo. Tito and Daisy had waited two weeks to go on their honeymoon; they wanted to help me re-open Kendle's after the water pipe break that was caused by, *who* knows, back in December. We had so much to do to open back up.

They didn't mind, and they told me they received a better deal on their trip by going in late January. So, the day after we had our grand re-opening, they packed up for a week and headed off to Catalina.

A few days later, I had to host a tour of the youth center with city officials and donors. The next day, Matt called me to tell me his fifteen-year-old sister Sara, had run away from home. She left her cell phone and a note saying she needed to just get away for a while! It has been two days since she left her Las Vegas home, where she lives with her folks. Matt and I called all of the friends she had here, but none of them had seen her since three years ago when she moved. Matt flew out to Las Vegas the next day to be with his parents.

I had called Paul to give him a heads up that even though Sara's friends haven't had contact with her, I thought maybe just in case she decided to come back here, at least the police would know. I opened my front door, but before I did, I heard a noise.

I looked around, but I didn't see anyone in the courtyard. I let myself in right away and locked the door. I kicked off my shoes, went to the kitchen, put on the tea kettle, and selected a nice chamomile.

I put on some cozy PJs that I purchased from Frills Boutique, the beautiful lingerie and apparel store at the mall.

The softest cotton pink shorts and a matching pink t-shirt with little red hearts on them. I call them my Cupid jammies!

When my kettle called me, I poured a cup of tea and sat on the couch.

I kept thinking about Matt's sister running away, the poor girl. I met her a month after Matt and I met. His parents and Sara had just moved to Las Vegas; she was just a 12-year-old kid.

Thin and long blond hair, bright blue eyes, with a love for butterflies and music. We went for a weekend visit, and she clung to me like a child with her favorite toy.

She asked me about clothes and my car, which she absolutely loved! I gave her a ride a few times, and over the years, I always gave her a Christmas gift, a gift card, or cash with a bracelet or some kind of butterfly jewelry.

Matt told me one time that I was her favorite because I sang, and I was cool, and that she wanted to have a car just like mine. I decided to send Matt a text and ask him if anything new had come up.

"Hi, Matt,

I was wondering, have you heard from Sara yet?

Your parents must be worried sick. Keep me posted

Nikki"

He quickly responded.

Hi Nikki,

*My parents said hi. As for Sara, my folks said she
has done this twice before and ended up staying with a friend of
hers in Rancho Niguel.*

*The whole neighborhood is aware, and all of her friends here
say they haven't seen her. She hates Vegas and the fact that my
folks moved her away from Rancho Niguel.*

I'm going home tomorrow, my parents think maybe.

*She went to my brother's houses in Thousand Oaks, or maybe she
is headed for Rancho Niguel.*

*Anyway, I'll be back tomorrow at 10 am
is there a chance you can pick me up from the airport?
If not, don't worry, I can catch an Uber or a Lyft."*

I text him back.

"Sure, Matt, I can pick you up. 10 am, right?"

He then responded.

*"Yup, I just have a carry-on duffel bag, so I should be outside by
10:05 am. Thank you, Nikki."*

I replied with a thumbs-up emoji. I tossed the phone and turned on
the news. One of the last segments spotlighted upcoming events in
the area.

"This Friday, music group Cold Creek will be in town for three nights, featuring lead singer Freddie Santana. The show is sold out for Friday and Saturday nights, but you can still get tickets for Sunday night. But hurry, there are just a few left."

That would have been a cool concert to go to, with everything going on, I didn't even know Cold Creek was performing here. Sunday, I knew I would be at Kendle's. Oh well, I'll have to catch a concert next time.

The next morning, I picked up Matt right on time.

"Hi, how was your flight?"

"Bumpy." He tossed his navy blue duffel bag in the back seat and slid into the passenger seat, pushing it back to give him more legroom.

We headed off down the road, under the isle of palm trees. Tall and lightly blowing in the wind, I never get tired of these trees.

"Thank you for picking me up. How about Stella's Coffee Shop? I'm starving, it's on me."

"Ok, I don't turn down a free breakfast. So, how are your parents holding up?"

"Oh, you know, they have seen this before with Sara. My mom said Sara has changed from who she was a few years back. She has a wild streak now; she dyed her hair, and apparently, she thinks she knows everything, and everyone is ruining her life, a typical teenager." He rolled his eyes and stated casually.

"Where do you think she could have gone?"

"My parents think that maybe she is headed back to California, but she would have to take a plane or a bus; she only has her learner's permit."

We arrived at Stella's Coffee Shop and took a booth in the back. This place is good for breakfast, lunch, *and* dinner.

The menu is like your typical diner food with blue plate specials for dinner, like fried chicken, meatloaf, and chicken pot pies. It's cute, and it has an updated farmhouse decor in light blues and peaches, like 1980s country, but more modern.

The waitress came by in a light blue uniform dress with a white apron around her waist. She pulled a pen from her hair and took our order on a notepad.

"What'll ya have, sugar?" She asked Matt.

"I'll take the Denver Omelet with cheddar cheese and whole wheat toast, please, *and* a cup of coffee."

"That comes with home fries and a cup of fruit, too!"

"Sounds good."

"And you little darlin'?" She turned to me.

"I'll take coffee and hot cakes and bacon with scrambled eggs."

"Ok, I'll put this in and be right back with your coffees." She smiled and walked away.

We returned to our conversation about Sara.

"So tell me, Matt, how would Sara be able to come here to California? Would she take a flight, an Uber or Lyft, or maybe have a friend who might have given her a ride?"

"My dad thinks she probably took a bus; she paid cash because her Debit card hasn't been used. The bank said she made a withdrawal of $800.00. The day before she left."

"That won't get her too far, so maybe a bus sounds more practical."

Our coffee arrived, and I packed mine with three sugars and cream. Yummm sugar!

Matt took his black.

"The thing I don't understand is why she would run away. My parents let her come to visit anytime, and she just has two more years of high school; she can move down here when she graduates." Matt looked perplexed.

I had to tell Matt right away; I think I know the answer to this, and it usually involves a person that you are head over heels with.

"Matt, do you think it has to do with someone she likes?"

"You mean a boyfriend?" He looked like a worried father now.

"Maybe, that might be a possibility!" I replied.

He turned it over in his head; I could tell the wheels were burning.

Then he was like Sherlock Holmes coming up with who dun it!

"You're right, she's hung up on some dude! He probably lives

here, and that's why she's so mad about living so far away.

Why didn't I think of that?" He said, thinking it was so obvious

that he hadn't considered it before.

"'Cause you're a guy!" I smiled.

  "Young love is very powerful."

I added.

"She's just a kid." Matt chuckled.

"She's fifteen; she's not a little girl anymore."

"That's true." He was serious now, his smile turning into a frown.

Our food arrived, and we ate.

Chapter 2

Kiss Me

After breakfast, Matt and I went to his house. I was just going to drop him off, but he wanted my opinion on his new surround sound and his new gym.

He tossed his bag in the hallway, and we went upstairs to the game room/movie room.

"Wow, you have made some changes, you put a bar in here with a big TV and a card table, and is this putt-putt golf?"

"Yeah, I can work on my golf game as I watch football."

"Oh yeah, that gets my vote."

He turned on the sound system and turned on the TV to his music app.

"Your card table is nice, did you get that in Vegas?"

"I did, last month, I went to see my folks, and I bought it from a guy who liquidated an old casino on the strip."

"It's cool, when is our first game?"

"Anytime, just give me a call."

He selected some rock music, such as "Ain't Talking 'Bout Love" (1978) by Van Halen. He turned it up loud; I could feel the walls vibrate from the music. It was so cool! He turned down the volume, and we walked out of the room to the hallway.

"I have it piped into all of the rooms, but if you don't want to listen in whichever room you're in, you can use the phone to turn it off. So in my guest room, you just go to the app on my phone, and you tap guest room, and boom, it turns it off in the guest room." Matt was like a little kid with his new toy, a boyish grin on his tanned face.

"I like that, I need one of these," I said, complimenting the sound system.

"Nikki, why don't you buy a house?"

"I've been thinking about that a lot; it's on my list."

The next song to play was "Why Can't This Be Love." Another one of my favorites from Van Halen.

Matt and I sang along and imitated playing guitars and drums. Fake banging our heads and dancing like rock stars. When the song was over, we busted out laughing.

"This speaker is fun, I'll have to get one right after I buy a house."

"I'm very satisfied with my purchase," Matt replied.

"So what are you going to do with the two other rooms you have?"

"I have a guest room already, so I was thinking of a home gym, but my stuff for that is in the third garage. I don't know, what do you think I should do with them?"

"See, that's the problem with buying a house with five bedrooms, a bonus room, and a three-car garage for one person, it's like you're living in a hotel."

"I love the house, and I got a great deal on it; I just couldn't pass it up."

"Well, let me think. You have three bedrooms just sitting empty. Do you need an office?"

"No, I do everything at work, so there's no need for one here." He replied

"Ok," I said, so I had my mind spinning about what to do with the extra rooms. "If it were me, I'd have a music room, but you don't play any instruments." He shook his head no.

"A hobby room, maybe to store your hobby stuff." I pointed out.

"My garage has my motorcycle and my truck, my hunting and fishing gear, besides my game room, that about covers it for my hobbies."

"I'm stumped then; I guess maybe you could get married and have some kids."

"Is that an invitation?" He smiled.

"No."

I shook my head, smiling.

We both laughed at our dark humor.

"Don't tease me, girl." He laughed.

"I'm not teasing, I'm telling the truth," I smirked, being silly.

"Oh yeah," Matt began to tickle me, and I returned it to him. By this time, we were laughing and poking each other in the arm and the shoulder. Then he used a wrestling move on me, and we ended up on the carpet. We rolled down the hall to the song "The Warrior" By Scandal. We started wrestling and getting one up on each other. The next track played was "Feels Like the First Time." By Foreigner.

Then we stopped wrestling, we looked into each other's eyes, and then we embraced. Passion ran through my veins like a fever rising as we kissed each other. While our hands raced over one another, I had no other thoughts except the fireworks that were exploding around us that only I could see. His strong arms wrapped around me, and I felt safe and cradled in his love. It seemed so right, but it was so wrong. I was dating another person whom I care about a lot. Stop, I told myself, my voice of reason denying my desire to continue.

"Stop!" I rang out loud! I pulled away from our kiss and I put on the brakes! We held each other for a few seconds while we caught our breath. I lost control and let this go too far when I shouldn't have. Once again, I was in Matt's arms, kissing him. I spoke up first, fast to get up. "I need to get going."

He got up as well, and we straightened our clothing. I took a deep breath and walked downstairs.

Matt got a text message. He pulled out his phone and read

"We just got a phone call from Sara; she said she is fine, she's with a friend, and she will call us tomorrow."

He typed back

"That's good to hear; I'm glad she is safe."

I placed my hand on his.

"It's a good sign that she is keeping in contact with her family. Just give her a little time, she'll be back home soon." I reassured Matt.

"I want to know who this friend of hers is," Matt said, tucking his phone into his back pocket.

He walked me to my car.

"If she tries to contact you, please promise me you'll let me know."

"Of course, Matt, I would never keep anything from you, I promise."

He smiled.

"I guess I'll see you around."

Neither one of us wanted to talk about our kiss, so we just let it go.

When I got home, I got a call from the contractor on the youth center project. "Hello, Ms. Rodriguez, this is Sam Chavez. I need you to get down here. We have a problem."

"I'll be there in 10 minutes!"

When I arrived at the youth center site, the contractor was standing in front of his white Chevy truck.

"Mr. Chavez, what's going on?" The look on his weathered face wasn't good.

"You have to see it." We walked to the gymnasium, he opened the door for me, and when I walked in, I just about yelled! In fact, I think I did!

"Ms. Rodriguez, when we arrived this morning, we worked on rooms in the next part of the building, and then when we came to bring in the new bleachers, we saw this."

The basketball court's hardwood floor was vandalized with red paint thrown all over it; then it looked like someone took a rake and dragged it over the wood floor, leaving deeply embedded scratches and causing the wood to splinter and crack in some places. The basketball court/gymnasium floor was ruined!

"I can't believe this. Why?"

"We don't know why, but it looks like someone took some bolt cutters and broke in, and then they did this! I'm really sorry."

The look on my face sank lower to the ground. I didn't know if I wanted to cry or beat my fists against the wall. Why did someone or some individuals do this?

"How long will it take to replace the floors?" I asked Sam.

"It's a four-day delay if we have the wood in stock. If not, we're looking at 4-6 weeks of delay.

"What!"

Disappointment in my voice.

"I can let you know by the end of the day, my floor guy will tell me if they have enough to cover the gym."

"Ok, have you called the police?"

"Yes, he did." Paul came in right behind me; I turned to him.

"I'm so glad you're here. Can you believe this?"

"This is crazy,"

he said, looking at the destruction before us.

Detective Sonya Smith came in right behind Paul

"Hi Nikki, Oh my word!" Was her reaction.

"Hello, Detective Smith."

She looked around at all of the mess before us.

"This is terrible. I'm sorry to see this," She responded with a look of complete sorrow on her face.

"Sonya, can you interview Mr. Chavez?" Paul asked her.

"Sure. Mr. Chavez, come with me."

They went outside, and then Paul embraced me

"How are you holding up?"

"I... Uh, I don't know, the good news is that we can fix it, but it's just so crapy! Why would someone destroy the youth center like this?" We parted, and he walked around to get a good look at the scene.

"What is it?" I asked, following him. I stood right next to him, wondering what was bothering him.

"There aren't any footprints, so I think the vandal scratched up the floor first, then poured the paint so they wouldn't have to step in it, so to speak. Smart! Plus, the paint seeps into the cracks and destroys any chance of saving it."

"Some criminals are good at covering their tracks," I remarked.

"Nikki, this is what we call rage! Whoever did this is very angry and dangerous!"

Chapter 3

Sweet

I headed back to Kendle's after leaving the youth center. I walked in and asked Ken, my part-time assistant manager and local artist, for a glass of red wine. "Tough day, boss?" He asked, wiping down the bar with a white bar mop.

"You won't believe what happened!" I put my purse on the bar and put my hand on my head; I was getting a headache.

Roxy came out of the kitchen with a box of vases, small, clear glass, with a single red rose in each one. She works part-time at her lab job, and she can manage her hours there, so she offered to work some shifts for me while Daisy and Tito are out of town this week. We decorated the place with red paper hearts that hung from the ceiling with red sparkling ribbon tails hanging from them. At the front desk, a small marble statue of Cupid shooting his arrow sat at the entrance. I bought it from Martin and Oliver's gallery last month. It's the cutest little cherub.

"Thank you for getting the flowers, I completely forgot," I told her, helping with displaying the vases.

"No problem, girly, you seemed to have a lot on your plate." Roxy smiled.

We were back to the usual uniform of black slacks and a white dress shirt; only we added red and pink striped neckties for the guys and pink and red striped neck kerchiefs for the gals. "Roxy, I was just about to tell Ken what happened!"

I filled them in on today's vandalism at the youth center, the police, and the possible delay.

"Oh no, boss, I think someone is trying to sabotage you. Remember when you had the tour at the youth center, and someone accidentally knocked over the punch fountain? I don't think that was an accident!" Ken said, with his eyebrow raised, he handed me my glass of red wine.

"Ken, that's right, I forgot about that."

"Nikki, I wonder if it's not kids pulling a prank or maybe a gang that doesn't want you or the youth center to become a thing!" Roxy said as she placed a vase on each table.

"All good points to consider, guys."

"What does Paul think?" Ken asked.

"He thinks it's a person with a lot of rage!"

"After what you just told us, I believe him!"

Roxy chimed in.

"Hey, not to change the subject, but what's going on with Matt's sister? Did they find her yet?"

"She is in contact with her parents, she needs some space right now, and said she's safe. The police in Vegas said as long as she is talking to them, that's a good sign."

I looked at my watch: 11:30 am. "Ok, let's open for the lunch crowd." We manned our stations, Ken at the bar, Roxy at the hostess desk (I need to hire another hostess), I reminded myself. The servers in the kitchen were ready to wait on customers, and I was managing this afternoon.

As I opened the door, I had a group of three men waiting; they were dressed in jeans and t-shirts that said, STAGE CREW.

"Welcome to Kendle's, please come right in."

Roxy sat them in a booth by the window.

Roxy came over to me and whispered, "I bet they are the road crew for Cold Creek!"

"Oh, that's right, they are in town."

"Heck yeah, Freddie is a local, he grew up here in Rancho Niguel."

"I knew that," I replied.

The server handed them our regular menu and our seasonal specials, filled with two new dishes added in each category on the menu that we developed, Chef Stark and I.

It came to this lovely addition of unique combinations and flavors.

Appetizer

Fig and Goat Cheese Crostini - *Goat cheese, with sautéed minced shallots, on crostini topped with diced figs in lemon juice and tarragon, drizzled with honey*

Bacon-wrapped Dates- *smoky pepper bacon wrapped around plump, sweet dates, broiled, and then drizzled with honey and crushed pistachios.*

Salad

Spinach Pomegranate Salad- *Fresh baby spinach leaves topped with feta cheese, candied walnuts, and pomegranate seeds tossed in a light champagne vinaigrette.*

Arugula with Currents- *Fresh sprigs of arugula, julienne carrots, Goat cheese, currents, and crunchy slivered almonds. With a light olive oil balsamic dressing.*

Entrees

Quail in Rose Petal Sauce- *sautéed quail in rose petal sauce sprinkled with red rose petals, served with mashed potatoes and baby peas.*

Four Cheese Ravioli In Truffle Cream Sauce- *Ravioli filled with ricotta, parmesan, romano, and pecorino. Covered in Black Truffle cream sauce, sprinkled with fried pancetta and basil*

<u>Dessert</u>

Chocolate Chili Cake

Chocolate cake infused with cayenne pepper, topped with homemade vanilla ice cream and fresh raspberries.

Cupid's Crème Brûlée- *vanilla bean custard, topped with sugar and torched until golden, with a pink tart cherry glaze drizzled on top.*

One of the road crew guys commented, "I'm getting the quail in rose sauce, that's rock n'."

"I'll take one too." Another roadie replied.

I smiled. I knew this menu was a kick, so I walked back to the kitchen. I smiled, giving him a thumbs up,

"Chef Stark, I think the menu is a hit."

"Awesome!" He shouted.

Tonight was a full house; Little Black Dress was performing again. It had been several weeks, but we sounded fantastic, as if we never left the stage for a month and a half.

We opened with "Barracuda" by the amazing group Heart, and we had a few rockers in the dining/bar lounge area.

I was half expecting some Zippo lighters to appear. Maybe later!

When we broke for our dinner break, I reviewed a text from Sam, the contractor,

"Nikki,

Good news: my supplier for the floors came through

I can pick up the wood tomorrow morning and have

the floors installed in three to four days."

"Sweet! Thank you, Sam." I responded.

We went back on stage and sang "Nothing But a Good Time" By Poison. Dana played her guitar like a pro. After 9 pm, our songs were geared more toward the romantics. We started with "Crazy Little Thing Called Love" by Queen. We played quite a few different love songs. "Under the Bridge" By Red Hot Chili Peppers is one of my favs, too! and "Run to You" By the amazing Bryan Adams. That song is so cool!

We ended the evening singing "Faithfully" by Journey.

"Thank you, ladies and gentlemen, thank you for being here at Kendle's this evening. Have a safe drive home."

After the customers dispersed, we began to pack up our instruments when a man casually dressed in jeans, a Hawaiian shirt, and a baseball cap and glasses walked up to us.

"I just want to say your band is fantastic. I enjoyed your sound. I was told this was the band to see, and I agree."

We had all looked up from what we were doing to see none other than Freddie Santana giving us accolades.

"You're Freddie Santana!" I said, surprised by his presence

I shook his hand, and so did the rest of the girls. He was taller than I thought; he still looked the same as he had back in the late 1970s, just with long grey hair and a few pounds heavier.

"Can we jam with you?" Roxy asked.

"Sure." He shrugged his shoulders.

Dana handed him her guitar and grabbed a spare. Emily grabbed hers, Roxy went back on drums, Taylor went to her keyboard, and I grabbed the mic and sang one of Cold Creek's most famous songs. Ken, Chef Stark, the servers, busboys, cooks, and Paul were our audience. It was a blast.

Freddie had a great time, too; he seemed so down-to-earth and cool. After three songs, we called it a night.

"Nikki, you and your band have to come to my concert, be my special guests."

"Heck yeah."

We all said. Freddie gave us the information we needed to get in and said he would have special passes for us for Sunday's show.

"Sweet, thank you. We can't wait!"

I said.

"Take care, ladies, see you Sunday, and thank you for the jam session, I enjoyed it."

He walked out of Kendle's a happy dude.

Chapter 4

Wonderful

Friday Morning, I got up early, I had to go to the Youth Center and select some decorative elements for the classrooms and the music room. I called Roxy and asked her to meet me there in half an hour; I told her I would bring coffee.

"Nikki, I'll take a raspberry mocha and make sure I get a quad shot in there."

"Ok, you'll be wired until next Tuesday!" I told her.

"Sounds good, girl, see you there."

I laughed at my crazy bestie.

I walked into Starbucks; I spotted Jessica setting out some pink and red thermal mugs and water bottles. She had the place decorated with pink and red hearts and silhouettes of Cupids. As a general manager, she does a wonderful job with her store.

Her employees love her, and she makes the store so warm and enjoyable. Although today, the weather was a nice 67 degrees, and that ain't bad for a nice February morning.

"Hey, Jessica."

"Nikki, I heard about your jamming session with Freddie. How was that?"

"We had a blast, and we get to go backstage with VIP passes to the concert on Sunday. Freddie gave us ten tickets, and one has your name on it, so you're coming with us."

"Oh my gosh, thank you, Nikki, oh my gosh, what am I going to wear? I need to get some of those ripped jeans at Abercrombie."

She walked behind the counter, came back down to earth, and took my order.

"I'll take a venti quad shot raspberry mocha for Roxy and, for me, a grande white chocolate Americano."

"Coming right up. Oh, this is going to be so much fun."

She was giddy now.

"Did you also hear about what happened at the Youth center?"

I asked her.

"Yes! Paul was in earlier, and he told me what happened. Nikki, you need to watch your back, or you might have a repeat of last summer!"

"You have been talking to Paul."

"Nikki, he's right, first the incident at Kendle's and now this! I don't think it's a coincidence."

"I know I put a new bottle of pepper spray in my purse."

"Look, I'll keep my ears open, but stay safe."

She said.

"Thanks, I will, and don't forget to meet me outside the Mission at Rancho Niguel around 7 pm, and then we can go in together."

"I'll be there." She was ready to rock, and she made the rock symbols with her hands, "Cold Creek, here I come."

After leaving Jessica, I was on my way to the Youth Center. When I got there, Sam, my contractor, and his team were working on prepping the gym for the wood to be put in.

"Good morning, Sam."

"Good morning, Nikki." Sam waved and went inside the gym; I figured I'd catch up later with him. I walked into the building, and Roxy greeted me.

"Hey girl, thanks for the caffeine, how much do I owe you?"

"Forget it," I told her, waiving my hand.

"Thank you." She replied with today's lipstick, "Be my valentine." A light reddish/pink. I remember when she bought it at Macy's. Some of the light renovations were done, including new windows, crown molding, light fixtures, a large lobby area, and a check-in desk with security.

I had it all planned out, the security measures so that each child would be on file with a photo and their emergency contact information. Each youth gets a key chain or a bracelet that they swipe, and then have a special secure password they punch in on the keypad at the desk to let them in. When a child leaves, they must be picked up by a registered adult parent, family member, or guardian. The photo of the family member or guardian is on file so that we can verify it, and the adult picking up must use their secret code to punch in on the keypad. The younger kids have their bracelets or keychains and have a special word they tell us at check-in, and we bring up the file on the iPad to verify it, with the same security as the older children. Hopefully, it works out with no problems.

"Roxy, I need your advice," I asked her with a look of concern.

"What happened?" She looked at me skeptically!

"Matt and I had a moment of..."

I spilled the beans to my bestie about my little romantic wrestle mania event, and finally, I asked:

"What should I do? Should I break up with Paul? I feel so guilty! He doesn't deserve that."

"Slow down, you kissed, that's all. You put the brakes on. Just leave it, don't say anything, move forward, and stay away from Matt. If you care for Paul, keep yourself away from Matt!"

"So you're saying pretend it didn't happen?"

"I'm saying don't tell Paul and stay away from Matt if you want to be with Paul. If not, then break up with Paul and go to Matt. You're at the point now where you have to make a choice."

"You're right; I know what I have to do."

"Nikki, where do you want these sofas?"

The decorators arrived and brought in the furniture for the teen room.

"Right over here."

I led them down the main hall to a yellow door that read TEEN ROOM. 13-17 years old only, they brought in two red sofas and placed them in the lounge area of this large room.

We filled it with a big TV, velcro darts on one wall, and a vending machine with soda, juices, water, snacks, chips, crackers, and candy. We had two Star Wars pinball machines, some phone charging stations for Android and Apple, and high tables with stools, more like a hang-out room when the teens are not in activities or classes. Next, Roxy and I added some Exit signs to some of the other rooms, hung some pictures in the lobby, added some fire extinguishers to classrooms, and filled the kitchen pantry with some essentials.

The day went by fast, and before I knew it, lunch had passed. It was 2:30 pm, and by now, I was starving, and so was Roxy.

We walked out of the building and headed to the bug to grab a burger at In-N-Out when Paul walked up to me, and Stacie stood by the truck door. Obviously, they came together in his truck.

"Hi Paul, we were just going out to get lunch."

"Hi, hun!" Paul kissed me on the cheek.

"Hi Roxy, I ran into Stacie at the department, and she asked me if I would drive her over here. She is meeting Mayor CJ, and they want to see the progress."

Just then, the mayor arrived in her chauffeured black Lincoln, which pulled into the parking lot.

Stacie just waved at me and Roxy but stayed by Paul's truck.

"How about I go with you two? I'm off duty." He offered.

"Ok, that sounds great." I smiled.

"Oh, my word! It's nearly completed, it looks wonderful!" The mayor shouted!

New plants and flowers decorated the entrance and the stone walkway. I led them all into the facility, and Stacie glared at me the whole time. I showed them the new teen room, the library, the homework area, the under-12 lounge, the playroom, and the nap area for the littles. The music room and the kitchen.

"All of the other rooms are ready. We just decided to keep them closed because they are finished and ready to go.

Every lounge, teen room, and playroom will have four instructors or adult volunteers at all times. Paul and the department have finished all background checks and fingerprints on the staff and volunteers, and two cameras are in every room and are up and running. Parents and guardians will be able to go to the app and see their children in the classrooms at all times.

We also have two plain clothes resource officers stationed in the facility at all times. Security for the children in the community is of the utmost importance."

"You've thought of it all, everything looks fabulous!? Mayor CJ was on happy pills today; her dark brown 1960s hair flip made her look like a deranged Sandra Dee. Lady, please! Don't disrespect the flip or my girl Sandra Dee, ugg...

She ran from room to room like a wild teen, the plastic smile screwed on her face, never moving.

Oh, honey, slow down on the Botox! Stacie, on the other hand, as much as I didn't like her, was pretty quiet and rolled her eyes every time the mayor said:

"WONDERFUL !!" I don't like you, Stace, but I'm right there with ya! I rolled my eyes, too, when she said it again and again after she saw the security features of check-in. "WONDERFUL!" Stacie looked like she wanted to strangle her.

I think Paul had tuned everyone out. He was on his phone texting someone.

"So that completes our tour."

"Well, you have outdone yourself, Ms. Rodriguez, and I can assure you that on the grand opening day, I will have the press here. Stacie has scheduled an interview with Local Five News, and I have asked for a national news reporter on this story, so Flame Phillips will be here too."

"My good buddy Flame, awesome," I replied.

"Yes, he's going to be in town for a family member he is visiting, and I had Stacie call him out in New York and ask him to come to our grand opening. I wish I had known that Flame is such a good friend of yours, I would have just asked you."

She casually said.

I could see steam coming from Stacie's ears now, and I admit it, I did chuckle, but Ms. Mayor thought it was from her comment."

"Just let me know next time, I would be happy to talk to Flame." I told her.

She flipped her hair and led Stacie down the hall, "Now, Stacie, this is what I'm thinking of for the grand opening." Stacie began to take notes in her purple notebook. Roxy looked at me, eyebrows raised, but didn't say anything.

When we got outside, the Mayor had a million ideas in her head, and they were now expelled as Stacie was rushing to take everything down.

"Paul, are you ready to go to lunch?" Roxy asked.

"Yeah, let's go, guys." We followed him to his truck.

"Stacie, we're going to lunch," Paul said, opening the door for me.

"Ms. Groves, I came with Paul; he's my ride." She kindly told the mayor.

"Don't worry, I'll drop you off at home we can go over my next idea for the photoshoot next week." Before Stacie could complain, the door to the Lincoln was opened, and she was ushered inside, but not before I saw the look on her face; she scowled at me again. Paul's back was to her, so he didn't see it. They drove off right away, and we went to lunch.

Chapter 5

Lights Out

After lunch, Paul dropped Roxy and me back at the Youth Center. I told him I would be just a few hours, and then we could grab some dinner and maybe see a movie. Roxy went inside, and I had a chance to kiss Paul.

Roxy and I worked until 5 pm, but it was getting dark now, and we were ready to leave.

Sam came into the kitchen as we put the last chair on the island that was in the middle of the room.

"Ms. Rodriguez, I just wanted to know if you want to see the floors. We started on one side, and we will be back on Tuesday at 9 am, but if you'd like to take a look before I lock up.

"Of course." Roxy and I walked to the large gym on the other side of the outdoor garden, and through the double doors, we saw workers putting tools in their trucks and picking up the last of their equipment. Sam walked us in and had us stay on the brown paper they rolled out over the finished section of flooring. He pulled back a small section of the paper to reveal a new wood floor.

"I love it, Sam, it looks really good."

"Very nice," Roxy replied.

"We should be finished by late Tuesday, and then we can sand it. The Painter should be here on Wednesday morning to paint lines on it for the court. Then we seal it!"

"This is great, so it will be ready for the grand opening next week." I felt pretty confident that now everything was coming together. Roxy looked at her smartwatch. Nikki, I have to head out. I'm going out tonight." She smiled.

"Sure, oh, thank you for all of your help today." I hugged her.

"Do you want me to wait for you? I can tell Mr. Perfect I'm going to be a little late," Roxy asked.

"No! I'm actually right behind you; I just have to go back inside and get my stuff and lock up."

"Ok, I'll see ya." She walked out.

"Sam, have you seen the other nail gun?" One of his workers asked.

"I thought you packed it up," Sam replied.

"I thought I did, but I can't find it." Sam's employee responded.

"Reggie probably packed it up. Go and ask him."

Sam pointed.

"He just left, but you're right, I think he did."

The employee stated confidently.

Sam and his workers began to finish laying out the paper to cover the rest of the floor.

"I'll see you on Tuesday, Nikki. We will be about fifteen minutes, and then we will be out of here."

"Ok, Sam, have a nice weekend."

"You too, Nikki!"

I left the gym and went back to get my black Tory Burch business bag; I had left it in the lobby. I checked all of the rooms to make sure the lights were out. I checked the bathroom, and the lights were off, so I headed towards the lobby. And then I heard a noise come from the kitchen. I opened the door to the classroom/kitchen, turned on the lights, and saw that a few cans had tumbled out of the pantry, the door partially open, exposing the shelving.

Three cans of tomato sauce lay on the floor, one rolled down to the fridge. After I picked them up and placed them back on the shelf in the walk-in pantry, the lights in the kitchen went out!

I pulled my phone from my bag and turned on the flashlight.

I closed the door to the pantry and headed to the fuse box at the end of the kitchen, behind the back door.

I opened the panel and hit the breakers, but nothing happened. A cold chill made the hairs on the back of my neck go up. Oh man, now what! This is all I need: electrical problems. I walked out of the kitchen, closed and locked the door to it, and walked back to the lobby. It was 5:30 and already super dark outside. I figured maybe I could catch Sam.

I was about to head out, but I dropped my phone when I bent down to pick it up. I heard what sounded like a projectile in my direction. It hit the wall behind me. I turned off my light and crawled behind a chair. Someone was in the room with me!

I could hear the sound of the nail gun and someone trying to make it work, but it sounded like it was jammed.

I got up and tried to run for the door, but, being so dark in here, I tripped on an end table and went flying over another chair. I put my hands out to stop myself, but I hit the floor hard.

My wrist was sore, and though I managed to get myself on my feet, I stayed low. In the fall, I had dropped my phone, and now I was searching for it.

I heard another nail hit the wall; the shot was about 10 feet to my left. Still moving my hand over the wood floors to find my phone, I could barely make out the table I knocked over. I roamed around there searching for my phone, and then my hand grazed over it, but it lit up, and then I took cover and crawled behind a chair.

The nail gun shot out again, a foot from my head. I left my spot and hid behind the fallen coffee table. The path to the door had no cover. I was an open target. What do I do now? So I decided to head to the kitchen. There was a back door there, or my other option would be the offices, which were closer to me, and there was a staff entrance, too.

I took a pillow from one of the plush lobby chairs and put it in front of me as a cover. I took my shoes off and put them in my bag. I made my way to the front counter and rounded it. I was behind it when another nail hit the chair I had just left.

I crawled quietly to one of the offices behind the lobby front counter. I made my way into one and closed the door. I clicked the lock and hid under the desk. I dialed 911! " 911 operator, what is your emergency?" *I'm Nikki Rodriguez. I'm here at the Youth Center on Bordeaux Ave. Someone is trying to kill me. Send help, please!* I went to my text messages and sent Paul a text: *HELP! SOMEONE IS TRYING TO KILL ME. I'M AT THE YOUTH CENTER, LOCKED IN AN OFFICE.*

"I'm on my way," Paul responded.

"Officers are on the way, Nikki." The 911 operator told me! I heard footsteps outside, walking around the lobby, but I didn't hear any more shots from the nail gun. I figured the assailant was looking for me. I crawled out from under the desk quietly and crept to the door. I stood at the side of the door, gauging whether or not there was someone on the other side.

Maybe the killer left, not being able to get to me. I didn't see any light under the door. Then again, maybe the killer was still close by, waiting, calculating my next move, silent and still!

I couldn't hear anything more except for the 911 operator telling me to stay put. I had my hand on the door, ready to release the lock.

All of a sudden, three nails came right through the door. I gasped and put my hand over my mouth to keep from screaming! I then stood away from the door, my heavy breathing now made my heart race. A thump, thump, it went, and I felt my neck pulsing rapidly, but now the door was being kicked! It was heavy and sounded like steel-toe boots! The top hinge fell off the door jam, and now the door hung sideways. I stood to the side of the room, away from the door, even though all I had was my pepper spray!

My heart pounding and my breathing coming in heavier now, I held onto my weapon, ready to spray my assailant.

The kicking was harder, and now the door flew off the last hinge. I pointed, and when the killer came into the office, I covered my face and sprayed and didn't stop spraying. The killer must have inhaled a large amount of the pepper spray because the attacker ran away, hacking and coughing.

I ran out, too; the smell of the lingering pepper was making me choke up, and it filled my eyes with tears, my mascara ran, and so did I!

The lights came back on, and I felt blinded by them. I didn't even see myself run into Craig and another officer.

"Nikki, Nikki, it's me, Craig, you're safe now!"

"Craig!" I cried and held on to him; I was shaking like a leaf.

"It's ok; It's ok, come on, sit down."

He led me to a chair, and I sat down, wiping my eyes. He gave me a handkerchief, and I dried my eyes.

The heavy smell of pepper spray lingered in the air.

Paul ran in.

"Nikki,"

He ran over to me.

"Anderson, you got her?"

Craig stood up.

"I'm going with Officer Yu to go look around."

He waved Craig on.

"Thanks, buddy."

Craig and Officer Yu ran to the offices and then to the back of the building with their guns in their hands.

"Babe, come here,"

Paul held me until I settled down, my adrenaline running over time.

"Can you tell me what happened?"

"I was closing up, and I heard a noise in the kitchen, and I saw some cans on the floor, so I put them away in the pantry, and then the lights went out, so I tried to hit the breaker, but nothing happened, and then I came out to the lobby, and someone was firing what sounded like a nail gun at me, I scrambled into one of the offices and called 911!"

My breathing was calmer now and almost back to normal.

Craig and Officer Yu came around the lobby again.

"Paul, we looked everywhere. Whoever was here is gone, and the back window was probably shattered by the nail gun that was left on the floor."

Craig said, pointing to the spot where the weapon was lying.

Other officers responded, and now we had a full team investigating.

My EMT friends James and Anita sat me down in the back of the ambulance and checked me out. Anita tended to my eyes.

"Here, I'm going to wash your eyes out with some saline." After she was done, she gave me a bottle of water to drink.

"Your throat might be sore for a while. When you get home, eat some ice chips. It will reduce any swelling you might have in your throat or on your lips. Other than that, it looks like you didn't get too much pepper spray on you."

James took off the blood pressure band.

"Blood pressure is normal now."

"Thanks, guys."

I pulled the blanket around my shoulders; it was quite chilly this evening. Paul walked over to me.

"Nikki, I'm glad you're ok!"

He smiled with those beautiful, jeweled greenish/blue eyes. He sat on the end of the ambulance with me, half in the bus and half out, with our legs on the bumper.

"So, the nail gun that was used to shoot at you was full. The safety was disabled, and that was how your attacker was able to fire it at you."

"The nail gun! One of Sam's workers was missing one; they thought another employee had put it away in the truck."

"We dusted for prints, and most likely, the only ones we find will be from the construction crew, but we will make sure they are all checked out, no stone left unturned. Someone *wanted* to kill you! After what happened in the gym, I'm afraid you're a target again, Nikki. Someone wants you dead!"

Paul took me home afterward, and he pulled a glass from my cabinet. Poured me some bourbon and set it right in front of me.

"I thought you could use something stronger than tea!"

"Thanks,"

I said, taking a drink. My red-rimmed eyes were sore from pepper spray and the crying.

I had cleaned my mascara off, but still, I felt like a mess. Paul sat down next to me and grabbed my hand!

"Nikki, I'm not letting you out of my sight."

Chapter 6

Let's Rock

Sunday finally arrived! I was ready to rock and roll tonight; I had it all planned out. I made my own ripped jeans from a pair that was ready for the trash. I tore out the knee area and frayed them; I made some rips in the thigh region, too. Next, I wore some black lace tights under my jeans to give them a nice look, peering through the holes. I frayed the ankle of the hem, and there I had an awesome pair of rocker jeans. I wore a black T-shirt with *classic rock rules* in hot pink writing. I ripped the collar of the shirt out and left it rolly and frilly. I cut the sleeves down and gave them a frayed look, too!

I put on my large silver hoop earrings and some silver bangle bracelets. I put on my sparkly, high-heeled black ankle boots, and there I was, little Miss Rocker. I put mousse in my hair and let my natural waves fall.

I tucked my cell in my back pocket and grabbed my leather jacket. I put my ID/credit cards and cash in my jacket pocket, and I was ready to go.

"Oh, I almost forgot my lipstick." I put on one of my favorite shades of hot pink and stuffed it in my jacket pocket.

"Now I'm ready."

I picked up Roxy, and we headed to the Mission at Rancho Niguel. The Mission is a new theatre that the city built last year.

It looks like a great big mission-style building, but inside, it has theatre seats and box suits. It also has a kick-ass food court, and it has a retractable roof. How cool is that? Tonight was a little chilly, so I didn't think the roof would be open.

Roxy was dressed in black ripped-up jeans and a black t-shirt; she had on a black leather jacket too.

"How are you holding up chicky?" She asked me.

"As well as can be expected with a person trying to nail me to a wall literally!"

"Yeah, well, you'll be with a lot of people tonight, so I wouldn't worry too much. I've got your back, girlfriend."

I chuckled, "Thanks, Roxy."

After we parked in the parking structure in section B of the Mission. Roxy and I walked to the entrance and met up with Jessica.

"Nikki, don't worry, babe, we've got your back."

"Thanks, Jessica."

I walked up to Will Call and gave my name.

"Nikki Rodriguez, I have some passes that are being held for me."

"Ms. Rodriguez, yes, how are you this evening?"

"Ready to rock."

"Awesome, here are your tickets. All you have to do is show these passes, and you'll be directed from there."

She handed me six passes in plastic holders with a long lanyard-style chain to slip around our necks. Dana, Emily, and Taylor walked up to us as we headed for the door.

"Ok, ladies, here are your passes."

I handed each girl her pass, and we high-fived,

"Here's to having a wonderful time tonight!"

Roxy said.

"Oh, please, don't say that word wonderful. '"

I replied with a stale sentiment to my voice.

Roxy laughed; she knew exactly what I meant. She filled in the other gals, and we laughed all over again.

"Ok, let's have a fun time!" She shouted.

Originally, we had two more passes, but Paul had to cancel. He said he had a meeting with the city council and the mayor, briefing them on the incident at the youth center.

I was bummed, but he said he would make it up to me. Chef Stark had a recital to go to for his niece at one of the high schools.

He told me it was a can't-miss event.

So it was just me, the band, and Jessica.

We walked in and were allowed to go backstage. Freddie and his band were hanging out in the lounge in their dressing room. It was cool, it looked like a mini club, there was a bar serving drinks, some velvet purple plush sofas, many mirrors around the room, and a lot of people hanging out around the band.

When Freddie saw us, he greeted us and introduced us to the other guys in the band.

"Ladies, Nikki, I'm happy you were able to come tonight."

"We wouldn't have missed it!" I replied.

"Let me introduce you to my band. This is Flick, this is Parker, that's T-bone over there, and this is Boss."

He introduced us to guys who were the same age as he was; they looked like a combo between the Stones and the guys from Kiss, without the makeup.

"This guy over here is our manager, Bobby."

His manager was a tall, athletic guy in his early 40s with gray hair scattered over his politician-style side part short cut hair.

"Ladies."

Was all he said while having his cell glued to his ear. He walked away and continued his conversation. We chatted with the band guys for a while. Dana and Emily played a few of their songs, and we laughed about current events in the world of rock.

After two Cokes, I asked Freddie where the bathroom was,

 "Right back here." He pointed behind another door by the set of vanity tables with lights atop.

Bobby, his manager, called him over, and they began chatting.

I went ahead and did what I needed to: washed up and checked my lipstick and makeup, fixed my shirt, and headed out.

I was walking back to our group when I heard voices coming from around a velvet purple curtain. I stopped for a moment and heard Bobby and Freddie discussing his not wanting to go on another tour. "Bobby, I'm tired. I need a break! I'm not as young as I used to be, you know."

"It's about maximizing your money on this tour; your ex-wife went and took over half of your worth."

"Jenny paid her dues; she deserved that money, she co-wrote some of my songs."

"The point is you need to be on the road; it's the only way artists make any cash now."

"What about an endorsement? You said we were going to do a commercial for Amazon."

"I'm working on it! But you need to add another city to the tour."

"No, and that's final!" Freddie stated and walked off in the other direction. I made it back to my party and mixed in.

"Well, ladies, you should make your way to your seats. We are going on in 15 minutes."

T-bone, the drummer said.

"Ok, let's go, gals!"

I said.

We wished them good luck, and we went to find our box suite.

"Wow! Fancy!" Taylor belted out a whistle after she gave her opinions on our suite.

We had a small lounge with a small buffet of appetizers, chips, salsa, wings, nachos, and some stuffed jalapeños. A small bar was behind the food, with a small beverage fridge filled with beers, wines, and soft drinks.

Our seats looked out to the stage in an eight-seat balcony. The seats allowed you to see the entire room; we sat alongside other separate suites, too! We waved to the guests on the left; they were with a company in the car sales business, Rancho Niguel Ford and Lincoln.

To our right, we had...

"Paul! What are you doing here?"

I had a look of surprise!

My thoughts were pure. *Are you friggin kidding me!* Standing right beside him was Stacie, and then Mayor CJ came to her seat holding a glass of Chardonnay. Two other city council reps were with them as well, holding red wine glasses.

"Hi, Nikki," Paul said, looking like the kid who got caught with his hand in the cookie jar.

I crossed my arms over my chest, waiting for an answer.

"Hi, Nikki,"

Stacie smiled with a wicked raised brow and a look of satisfaction coming to her mouth. She had her hand in the crook of Paul's arm.

"Um, Stacie, can you give me a minute?"

Paul asked her.

She smiled and then walked back to the lounge area of her suite.

Paul moved close to the glass divider to converse with me.

"Nikki, I know you're upset, but it's not what you think."

"I thought you had a meeting."

I told him with ice in my words.

"I did, and we had a meeting, but Mayor CJ invited me and two other council members to the concert; she wouldn't take no for an answer, and I came just to keep the situation cool."

"What situation?"

"The department needs some resources, and the budget is coming up next month."

"Oh, so now you're a politician for the department."

"The mayor had some questions about what the department needs, and I was happy to help. This is stuff we need to do our jobs."

He was doing his best to de-escalate my anger.

His face was innocent and void of any wrongdoing on his part. Even though he was selling plastic vomit like a five-and-dime store!

The lights went low to indicate that the concert was going to begin.

"Fine!" I gave in, dissipating my anger and changing my tone.

"I have to get to my seat." I politely told him.

"Can I meet you at your place after the concert?" He asked me

"Ok," I said, "Are you ready to rock?" I asked him.

"Yeah!" He smiled and looked so cool in his jeans and his black button-down shirt.

He reached over the glass barrier and kissed me. I smiled and then went to my seat.

The concert opened with a blast of lights and sparks raining down over the stage. The band appeared on a two-level terrace on the stage.

Their logo of Cold Creek, spelled out in green neon with a blue river in neon, lit up behind them. The large screens, four of them, showcased the stage and the performers up close.

Freddie came out in his signature blue jeans and a black t-shirt. His grey hair hung in wild waves while he played his famous red guitar. I had a glass of red wine and settled on having a great time at the concert.

A plate of hors D' oeuvres, two glasses of red, and one beer later, I was singing along with the other girls to our favorite songs. Paul looked over at me quite a few times; he looked like he wanted to be at our party instead of the mayor's.

For the grand finale of the concert, the roof opened, and we were treated to a show of fireworks. It was the coolest concert in my books.

When the concert ended, all of us were invited to have drinks with the band. I invited Paul to come with us, and he agreed and thanked Mayor CJ Groves for all of her hospitality.

He took my hand, and I saw Stacie give me another scowl behind Paul's back.

We went backstage and had a chill time; we had drinks, we talked, and then, eventually, we decided to call it a night.

"Bobby, where is Freddie? Paul and I are leaving, and I wanted to say bye to him."

"Freddie!" Bobby called out, searching the lounge for him.

"You're right, I haven't seen him for a half an hour. Hey Parker, where is Freddie?"

"I haven't seen him, man!"

"Well, if you can, just let him know I wish him all of the best."

"Yeah, sure thing, Nikki. Have a good evening."

He smiled and waved us on.

After I dropped off Roxy, Paul met me at my place.

"That was the best concert!" Paul remarked.

"I know, right? Oh, and by the way, I happened to get you this!"

I handed him a signed Cold Creek t-shirt."

"Thank you. I love it, Nikki!"

We stood by my front door, and he lingered with me, and then we kissed.

We heard a rustling by the teak benches.

"What was that?" I asked after pulling my smackers away from his.

"Here, go inside and lock the door."

I did what he said.

In about five minutes, he knocked on the door.

I checked the ring cam, and when I knew it was him, I opened the door.

"I looked around, but there was no one there."

He came in for a short while.

We didn't talk about Stacie or the mayor or the issue I had with him at the concert.

We had a cup of tea on the sofa, we made up over a long kiss, and then he said he had an early day, so he headed out.

"Keep your doors locked and use the Ring Cam. If you feel like someone is out here, call 911, and I'll be here as quick as I can."

"Ok, good night."

We went in for another kiss, and then he went home.

Chapter 7

Lost and Found

I turned on the news when I woke up around 7:30 am.

Last night, I forgot to ask Paul how the case was going with my attacker. For one night, I pretty much ignored it and had some fun. That was until Paul and I arrived at my doorstep and realized we weren't alone.

Someone *had* been outside in the courtyard, but that wasn't the only thing on my mind. I was still wondering where Sara was, and I thought of calling Matt to find out if he had heard from Sara again. Then I thought about our kiss at his place, and it seemed like a good idea to put some distance between us.

Today, I had lunch duty at Kendle's.

Tito and Daisy would be back in a few days, so I figured I might as well go and get some work done.

When I arrived at Kendle's, Chef Tony Stark had just arrived with his sous chef and two busboys.

"Good morning, everyone."

"I heard the concert was a blast, Nikki."

Chef Stark asked.

"Yes, it was. We missed you."

"I know, but I can tell you my niece was fantastic up on stage. I think she might be getting a music scholarship to college."

"That's really cool, Tony." I smiled.

The guys went to the kitchen, and I headed for the dining area.

We all went right to work. I opened the shades in the lobby and put out the menus. I made sure the tables all looked clean and ready for our first lunch customers.

An hour later, I opened the front doors to a few customers waiting out in the brilliant sunshine.

My lunch servers quickly came out with beverages and took lunch orders. Ken had everything going in the bar, not missing a beat.

Around 1 pm or so, the guys from Cold Creek came in.

"Nikki, hi, we didn't know you would be here."

Boss commented.

"I own this place," I replied and smiled.

"I knew there was a reason why I liked this restaurant,"

Flick said, taking a seat.

"We've been here twice before; I can't get enough of that chocolate chili cake,"

T-Bone said.

"So, where is Freddie?" I asked.

Parker leaned over to me.

"We can't find him, Nikki."

I had a look of astonishment on my face.

"What?"

"Yeah, we called him on his cell and tried his hotel room, but no one has seen him,"

T-Bone replied.

"We can't say much, yet Bobby told us not to spread it around, you know what I mean,"

Boss said, looking around to make sure no one heard our conversation.

"Ok, well, if you don't hear from him soon, call the Rancho Niguel police. My boyfriend Paul is a detective there; he is very good at his job."

"Thanks, love, we'll do," Parker replied.

I left them to enjoy their lunch, and I went upstairs to my office.

I dialed Paul's number, but I got his voicemail, so I left him a message.

"Paul, please call me as soon as you get this message."

A few minutes later, my phone rang a tune of "Hit Me With Your Best Shot" by Pat Benatar.

It was Paul.

"Hi, can you talk?"

"Briefly." He replied.

"I think Freddie Santana is missing."

"I know, I just spoke to his manager, there was a note left at the lobby for him, it read,

I'm taking time off! Don't try to find me!

I guess we have another runaway."

"Does Bobby know what time he left? Was it after the concert?"

"No," Paul replied.

"I overheard them discussing some extra concerts that Freddie didn't want to do. Do you think it had to do with that?"

I told Paul, remembering the heated conversation.

"I don't know." He replied.

After speaking to Paul about all of this, he said there's nothing he can do. Freddie left voluntarily, and he is of sound mind, so there is no crime. He said his manager insisted on the police department looking for him, but Paul said the department couldn't do anything; he suggested just letting him take some time, and he would most likely be back when he was ready.

Lunch today was busy, so by 6 pm, I was ready to go home. Roxy took the night shift for me this evening, and I told her I was headed home to enjoy a glass of wine and put my feet up.

"Have a good one, girly."

She waved as I left.

The mild temps outside this evening were 72 degrees, and no wind.

I had walked over here to Kendle's this morning, and so I walked back home.

 I was going to go and see Oliver and Martin, but then I remembered they were going to be out for the evening. I got to my door, and someone grabbed my arm just as I turned the key! I let out a shriek, but when I turned around, to my surprise, I came face to face with Sara.

"You scared me. What are you doing here?"

I asked her, opening the door for us.

"Surprise, I came to see you, Nikki."

She hugged me.

"Your parents and your brothers are worried sick about you."

She certainly looked different; she had dyed her shoulder-length blond hair a dark brown, and now she wore black eyeliner under her baby blues and also had on thick black fake eyelashes. Her burgundy lipstick matched her shirt, and she had a Coach handbag slung over her arm and a black duffle bag on the other arm. A short black skirt with black lace tights and black Doc Martins on her feet made her look much older than fifteen.

"I had to get out of Vegas; I hate it there! All of my friends are here." She crossed her arms over her chest.

 "I'm not going back!"

"Young lady, the first thing I'm going to do is let your parents know you are ok."

"No! You can't tell anyone I'm here. Especially my brother. He called our parents and told them I came here to see some guy, how did he know about Jagger?"

She said in defiance.

"Really?" I replied.

"Oh ... yeah, I should have known. My brother wouldn't come up with that on his own; men aren't that in-tune."

"Are you hungry?"

"Yeah!"

"Pizza?"

"Yeah." She smiled.

I called in a pizza with her favorite toppings: pepperoni, olives, and extra cheese. I went to my room to change, and when I came back, she was looking at the pictures on my fireplace mantel.

"So you got a new guy, huh?"

"I'm dating Paul Anderson; he's a cop."

"I know, he's the one I saw the other night when you guys were making out?"

"Yup," I replied, feeling embarrassed.

"He's cute, I'll say that, I don't blame you, my brother is a bonehead, he should have asked you to marry him a year ago."

She said, taking a seat at the dining table. She put her purse on the chair beside her and dropped her duffel bag on the floor.

"It's not him; it was me, I'm just not ready to get married yet."

I sat down across from her.

"Me too, I'm not getting married until I'm 30. I need that time to become me."

I smiled.

"So, do you have a place to stay?"

"I've been at the Holiday Inn on Mission Ave. I paid for the last three days, but I checked out today, I'm almost outta money."

"How much do you have left?"

"100 bucks."

"$800 took you this far?"

"I had some babysitting cash stashed in my room, about $400 bucks, then I went and took the rest out of the ATM."

"$1000.00 doesn't get you very far anymore," I stated

"Nope," she realized.

The bell rang, I checked the Ring cam first, and then opened the door for the pizza dude.

"Ok, dinner is served."

I put some plates on the table and took two Cokes out of the fridge.

While we ate, I asked her a few more questions.

"So, what are you planning on doing now?"

"I figured I'd try to get back into school here; maybe I can live with a friend of mine."

"Not with Jagger!" I told her.

"No, I have a few friends here I can probably stay with, just two years, and then I'm getting my own apartment."

"Is that right, and what are you going to do to pay for that apartment?"

"Now you sound like my parents."

"Come on, Sara, this is real life!"

She took a deep breath and exhaled, intelligent that she was, it did occur to her that she needed to be honest with herself about her future.

" I don't know, maybe I'll go to vocational school, I don't want to go to college; don't even try to change my mind."

She was very matter-of-fact about this issue.

"Ok, well, what do you want to learn at vocational school?"

She took another slice of pizza and put it on her plate.

"I was thinking phlebotomy, something in the medical industry. Blood doesn't bother me."

She took a bite of gooey cheese

"Ok, that sounds good, but even vocational schools cost money."

"I have a college tuition account that Mom and Dad put together for me when I was little. I have about 48k in there. I can use that."

"Seems like you have thought it through."

"Hmm, yeah."

She said, taking another bite of pizza.

"So you really want me to keep this from your brother?"

She wiped her mouth with a napkin and replied,

"Please! And I swear I will call my parents right now and tell them I'm staying with a friend, and I'll tell them that I will get a ride in a few days to Rancho Niguel. I'm just not ready for the drama from my parents.

The first thing they'll do is have Matt lock me up at his place until they get here. Just a few more days of freedom."

She begged.

"I promise, and then you can take me to Matt's house, and I won't fight you on it."

She held up her hand.

"I promise!"

"I can't believe I'm going to agree to this; you do know I'm dating a cop."

"He doesn't have to know. Besides, I'm visiting a friend."

"You ran away; you're a minor, I could get into trouble for this."

"No, my parents know where I am! I mean, in a way, they know I'm traveling to see a friend."

I thought this over: Paul will probably kill me, Matt will probably kill me, and Matt's parents will want to kill me.

"Ok, Missy, two days, and after that, you come clean."

"I will, I swear."

She smiled, giddy.

I knew I was going to regret this.

Chapter 8

Bad Ideas

When I woke up, I had a note waiting for me from Sara.

Jagger picked me up; we are off to the

Farmers Market,

I'll be back by noon.

Here is the number to my second phone

555-3456

I added her phone number to my contacts, and then I poured

myself a cup of coffee and indulged in some coffee cake in the

fridge. It looked a little empty, so I knew I had to stop by the store

to pick up a few things.

I got ready. It was warm out today, so I opted for a pair of navy

blue shorts and a white linen long-sleeve button-down shirt, open

with a white tank top underneath. I rolled up my sleeves about

three-quarters of the way and added some baby blue beaded

bracelets.

I slipped on my white Stan Smith Adidas tennis shoes and my navy

crossbody purse from Tommy Hilfiger.

I put the top down on the bug and headed to the store. I drove down the street, and on my way, I spotted a few people selling baskets filled with stuffed animals, candies, flowers, and balloons. They looked adorable.

Many people had side hobbies and sold them on the street corners, usually by the gas stations or entrances to the strip malls. It looked so festive, with a white easy-up for shade and so many baskets filled with cute Valentine's gifts. An array of pink, red, and white reminded me that I still hadn't bought anything for Paul for Valentine's Day.

I reminded myself to go out and shop for something, although I had no clue what to get.

I parked the car at Sprouts. I sent a quick text to Paul about seeing each other this evening, but he said,

"Poker night, babe. I tried to get out of it, but Chief wants to win back his $300.00 from Craig. I'll call you after the game."

Bummer, I thought, but I guess I can read that mystery I've been wanting to dive into. I put my phone in my purse, and I spotted a red Ducati in the parking lot. And I knew to whom it belonged. My first thought was to get back in the car and high-tail it to another store.

Stater Brothers is just up the street, and right now, I thought it was probably the best idea.

You're being ridiculous, Nikki. Why are you afraid to face Matt? The kiss we shared the other day was heavy on my mind. I had tucked it away for a while because, of course, I didn't want to believe it happened.

I had taken issue with my loyalty, where was it? Paul had been straight with me and a good guy; he didn't deserve this. And it was killing me that I was the one being dishonest.

I wrestled with this thought in my head until I just said to myself, always face your fears head-on. I had to discuss this with Matt, not here at Sprouts, but maybe at the park or the garden in the mall. That was it, the plan.

I walked into Sprouts, grabbed a shopping cart, and searched the store for him. I saw him putting strawberries in his shopping cart. I headed over to the strawberry section of produce and surprised him.

"Are you making Strawberries and Angel cake?"

He turned around with a smile.

"You know it's my favorite."

"With fresh whipped cream, oh, that sounds good right now."

"So what's new with you?" He asked.

He had on jeans and a white T-shirt, with his helmet, his Dainese motorcycle jacket, and a black OGIO backpack sitting on the top portion of his cart.

"Wow! That's an interesting backpack."

"It's shaped aerodynamically for motorcycle riders."

He showed me. He opened the large zipper of an almost empty pack.

"Pretty cool!" I responded.

"I have an idea: finish your shopping, I want to take you someplace," Matt told me.

This wasn't the plan!

I finished up shopping, and Matt said he would come by my place in half an hour. He also suggested I put on some jeans.

I went home, put all of the groceries away, and changed into a pair of skinny jeans.

I also hid Sara's tote bag in the hall closet. Now, if I have to go with him to see another house, all bets would be off, but I figured it would give me a chance to talk to him and be straight about not having close contact with him. Friends were fine as long as it didn't go past friendship.

He rang the bell a half hour later, "You're right on time."

"I just had to run my stuff back home."

"So where are we going?"

The suspense was building in me.

"One second." He went to my bedroom closet and brought out my black Perry Boots by Karl Lagerfeld Paris.

I just bought them; they are motorcycle boots, meets city boots, and they have a cute array of faux pearls on the top part of the boot. So stinking cute!

"What are you doing with those?"

I asked with curiosity.

"I need you to put them on. They're not ideal, but they'll do,"

He said, handing them to me.

"Ok." I sat on the sofa and put them on.

"Ok, now what?"

He moved to the coat closet.

"You'll need this too!"

He handed me my leather jacket.

"You do know it's 75 degrees outside."

He chuckled, "Follow me."

We went outside, I locked up, and followed him to the visitor's parking spot in front of my unit.

His motorcycle sat there with his black AGV helmet, and sitting next to it was another black helmet with red swoosh designs on the sides, an AGV K1 Warmup helmet, at least that's what Matt told me.

"This is for you," he handed me the helmet.

"I'm pretty sure it's the right size."

"You bought this for me? Whoa! You mean, we're going on this thing? Together?"

"Right behind me, there's a seat and some foot pegs."

He got on his Ducati and began to fasten his helmet.

I put the helmet on my head; it was a full-face one that had a shield over the eyes, which you could raise. It did fit perfectly, snug around the head and cheeks, covering my nose and mouth, and just having visibility for me to see.

Wait! Was I really doing this? I fastened the bottom strap and hopped on the bike. My seat was soft for its size and comfortable. I have to admit it was a very snug fit.

Matt's position made him lean over the engine. With my legs on the foot-pegs and my arms around Matt, I felt like a little koala bear sitting on and hugging her mom's back.

Matt started the motorcycle. "Are you ready?"

"No, yes, I guess so!" I said reluctantly,

"You'll be fine, trust me. Just remember that when I lean for a turn, lean with me."

"Ok." I held on tight to him, and we rode off.

It's not that I wasn't into trying new things, but seriously, a motorcycle! Was I crazy?

These things are so dangerous. What was I thinking? Off we went, cruising down the street at a normal speed.

I knew Matt didn't want to freak me out too much, and I knew he was taking it slow for me. At the back of my mind, I kept thinking this was a bad idea.

As we rode down the streets, taking a turn here and there, I thought of my promise to Sara. I felt bad for not telling Matt that his sister was staying with me, but it wasn't my story to tell.

I had promised Sara, and she said she would come through and tell her family.

Was I doing the right thing?

We rode up Red Hill Rd, going up to the hills, the same road that the house Daisy and Cat had rented last summer, but instead of turning at the stop sign, we went straight and climbed the hill. The ride was liberating: the turns, the breeze that went past us, and the speed. It was fun, and I found myself enjoying the ride.

We arrived at the plateau of the hill; the area was a well-known part for hiking and scenic photos. We parked the motorcycle on the roadside scenic stop site. When I took off my helmet, the view of the city down below us was breathtaking!

"Quite a view, isn't it?"

Matt asked me when he took off his helmet.

"Amazing! It's beautiful!"

We stood just admiring the scene, neither one of us saying anything, letting the beauty sink in.

The Sun, high above us, shining bright. The iridescent rays of warmth covered the city.

The blue sky was free from any pollution, clear and wholesome to breathe in.

"I was just going to say about the other day at my place."

He started with, but I interjected with my own opinion.

"I'm sorry about that; it's not my intention to mislead you. I had a moment of weakness, and I apologize."

I said, walking away and turning my back, I wasn't angry, but I was disappointed with myself.

Matt knew he had to tread lightly; I was known for bolting when the conversation became too intense.

"I just wanted to say, don't beat yourself up about it. I was the one at fault. You have been very clear that you are with someone else, and I should have put the brakes on first.

Until you come to me and tell me you want to be with me, I said I wouldn't pressure you, just let me take this one."

I felt bad; he was taking the whole cake here and letting me off the hook.

I turned around to face him, "Friends then."

 I smiled.

"Forever." He said and smiled.

"Come on, I want to show you the Youth Center; you'll be the first to see it."

He looked at me awkwardly as if to say what are you talking about.

"I'll explain when we get there. Let's go."

I said cheerfully.

We got back on the bike and rode over to the Youth Center,

Just before we pulled in, I could have sworn I saw Paul in his black unmarked charger going down Palm Drive, maybe not; there are so many of those Dodge chargers around here.

We pulled into a parking space in front of the building, and a few white trucks from Sam's crew were there, working on the finishing touches.

We dismounted the bike, took off our helmets, set them on the handlebars, and walked to the front door.

"So this is it!"

We went into the lobby, Matt looked around the room and admired the Spanish architecture, the high ceilings, the arched doorways, and the blue, yellow, and green Spanish tiles along the walls.

"This place is gorgeous! So, how are you connected to this?"

"My stepdad, Jeff, financed the project, and I sort of gained a position on the board."

"Good job, I think it's a great addition to the community, it's very much needed. Say thank you to Jeff for me. By the way, how are your folks?"

"They are doing well. They just got back from a short stay in Italy, and I'm going to visit them in a month or so. My mom said she has a surprise for me, who knows what she's cooking up."

"Tell them I said Hi."

"I will, thanks."

We walked around to the kitchen and then some of the classrooms. The art room already had easels, paints, supplies, and some drawing tables.

The pottery room had pottery wheels, tables, supplies of clay, cutters, paints, and a large oven. We looked over the teen room, and then we went out so that I could give him the tour of the baseball diamond and the tennis court.

Next, we went to the pool and lockers; then we arrived at the basketball gym.

Sam and his crew had just finished adding new locks on the doors, and the alarm and camera system were installed as well.

"Hi Sam, how's it going?"

"Hi, Nikki, you're just in time, we just started removing the cover on the new floor."

Matt and I stood at the entrance while Sam and his crew removed the thick brown paper that covered and protected the new floors. Underneath was a beautiful and shiny new court floor for the gym.

"Oh, Sam, that looks amazing. Your crew can work miracles."

Sam walked over to us and replied.

"Well, Nikki, considering the mess from the vandal. We had a lot to fix. By the way, did they catch that person who attacked you with my nail gun?"

"Not yet!"

I whispered, hoping he would drop the subject. I didn't want Matt to hear about another episode of someone trying to hurt me.

Too late!

"You were attacked by a nail gun. Why?"

He was confused and concerned.

"You didn't hear. Poor Nikki was working in the lobby, and someone tried to kill her with my missing nail gun. She hid in an office until the police arrived."

Sam was pouring out all of the chisme` (the Spanish word for gossip).

"Can you believe it, with my nail gun, I asked my foremen who was the one that left it lying around, I need to know.

The only people here that day were Nikki, Roxy, the mayor, that tall woman with the scary eyes, and Paul, the cop.

That was it! My guys are good, and none of them even know Nikki."

After Sam spilled the beans on my mishap, he turned to me.

"So, Nikki, what do you think of the alarm system and the cameras?"

"I think it was a good idea; we needed security here."

"I might get one for my place. I'm on two acres, and sometimes it can be very dark with all of the trees I have, so I think I'm going to get some of these too!" Sam stated.

"I guess we should be going now, thanks, Sam. The floor is magnificent."

I smiled, pulling Matt out of the gym.

"Thank you, Nikki. I take pride in my work, and I'm glad you are happy with it."

Matt was looking for more answers; he wanted to stay and chat more with Sam, but I led him back to the main building.

"You were almost killed? What's going on?"

"I don't know, Matt,"

I might as well give him the whole story.

"I was working in the lobby, locking up and getting my bag. Roxy had just left, and I told her I'd be right behind her. Then, as I was ready to leave, a noise from the kitchen made me go and check it out.

A few cans fell from the shelf in the pantry, and then the lights went out. We have had so many workers in here that I didn't think much of it, and I tried the breaker, but nothing happened. I went into the lobby, and that's when someone tried to kill me with a nail gun."

"These nail guns have a safety mechanism on them."

"Yes, they do, but someone disabled it. That's what Craig said."

"So this was someone specifically gunning for you?"

He asked.

"Believe me, I've been going over it in my head, and I don't have any enemies, I haven't upset anyone lately, and ..."

I trailed off, not knowing what to say.

My cell chimed a text song of Cupid's arrow hitting a target.

It was from Sara! "Just give me a minute, Matt."

I walked a few feet away from him to open and read the text.

"Hi, Nikki, I am in San Diego. Jagger wants to stay the night this evening and go to see that whale that's over here. I won't be home until tomorrow."

I was furious; now I had to play the wicked stepmom and tell her to get her hiney back here, or else it would be her brother Jagger would meet.

So I texted her back.

"Young lady, you need to come back this evening, NO staying with Jagger overnight, not on my watch. Your brother is standing five feet away from me; he is still so worried about you. I will keep my promise as long as you make good choices."

A few seconds went by, and then she texted me back.

"Ok, ok, I'll come back tonight, such a party pooper."

She left me an emoji with a crazy, silly face.

"I'll be there by 8:30 pm, promise."

"Ok, see you then,"

I replied.

I walked back over to Matt, and he began with,

"My mom got another call from Sara; she said she is fine and she will call them in a few days."

I smiled.

"See, Matt, she knows you guys are worried about her. She'll be home real soon, I can feel it."

Keeping Sara from Matt was getting sticky, and I knew making that promise to Sara was a bad idea.

"Can you run me back home, Matt? I have a few things to take care of."

"Sure, I have a few errands to run myself. Let's go."

We got back on the motorcycle, and Matt dropped me off at my front door.

"Here is your helmet back."

"That's yours, darlin'; maybe we can go for another ride sometime."

"Thank you. I guess I'll see you around."

He bid farewell and took off.

I went inside and hung my jacket in the closet, placed the helmet on the shelf in there, and changed my boots to a pair of Toms. Then, I decided to go down to Kendle's to get some work done.

About an hour later, I got a call from Paul.

"Hi, how's your day going?" I asked him.

He took a deep breath and let it out.

"For starters, I had an angry Matt wondering why I don't have anyone in custody for attempted murder for the nail gun incident, and if that wasn't enough, he wanted me to do a check on some guy named Jagger Rollins. It seems Sara spoke to her folks and said she, her friend Violet, and Violet's brother Jagger were hanging out together.

Matt thinks this is the guy she came to see. I told him there was nothing I could do, and then he walked out. By the way, did I see you riding on the back of that motorcycle of his!"

Oh boy, that *was* Paul that I saw! Yup, I knew it!

It was a bad idea!

Chapter 9

Did Someone Say a Biker Bar

My phone call with Paul didn't go well. I told him a little white lie, and I have to admit, I did feel bad about it.

He had cornered me, and I did what most warm-blooded humans do: I lied! I'm not proud of myself, but here goes.

When he asked me why I had been on the back of Matt's bike, I told him the bug wouldn't start and that I needed to get to the Youth Center and I was going to get an Uber, but Matt had stopped by when he saw me pull out of Sprouts with my hazards on, I had barely made it home when my car just died.

After he dropped me off, he waited to take me back home, and then he cleaned my battery terminals. Turns out they were preventing me from getting the car started.

Paul apologized and said he understood now and would help if the bug needed maintenance.

Crisis avoided!

I went downstairs to the restaurant to go over the details for the Valentine's Dinner later this week, February 14th was rolling around already. When I walked up to the bar, Ken said, "Nikki, someone is waiting to speak to you at booth 4."

I turned around and saw a guy with a baseball cap and jeans with a Def Leppard t-shirt on.

"Thanks, Ken."

I walked to booth 4, hidden partially by being in the corner.

"T-bone, what brings you here?"

"Hi, Nikki, me and the other guys were wondering if you had seen Freddie."

"No. I'm surprised he hasn't come back yet!"

"Yeah, we've gotten kinda worried now. I was wondering, since this is your turf and all, maybe you could keep an eye out and let us know if you see him. We just want to make sure he's ok."

"Sure, I'd be glad to help."

He slid out of the booth now.

"Thanks, Nikki, we appreciate it. Here is my number in case you run into Freddie. I hope he comes back soon."

He paid Ken for his beer, and then he gave me a wave.

"Bye," I replied.

I tapped my phone and went online to look up Freddie Santana; there were a few fan blogs that I checked out. A few had speculated over the reason for the concerts being canceled in Arizona, and their reasons varied.

One guess was that Freddie had kicked it, and they were waiting for the family to respond; another one had Freddie being taken by aliens just outside of Mesa. Another one said they spotted Freddie singing at an old biker club off Route 66 called Axels.

I decided to check out Axels. I phoned Jessica.

"Hi, Nikki."

"Hi, Jessica, are you free tonight?"

***

I picked Jessica up at 8 pm. Roxy was closing this evening, so she couldn't go, but at least Jessica and I could check this place out.

We dressed in all black with high-heeled boots and leather jackets. We had to blend in, right?

We arrived at a place that looked like it was on its last leg; the building was old, and the drab beige paint was peeling off the siding.

The neon sign in blue spelled out Axles, but minus the E and the L, so it read Axs! The parking lot was filled with Harleys of many different styles: Fat Boys, Softails, Sportsters, Road Kings, some low riders, and some Heritage classics, only because Jessica filled me in on the bike models.

"How do you know what these bikes are called?"

"I dated a guy who sold them over at Rancho Niguel Harley Davidson."

"That explains everything."

I told her.

We walked in and went to the bar. I have to say it was nicer inside than I thought it would be, modern with a vintage feel. The large oak bar took up the entire side of half of the place.

Clean and simple wood tables and chairs were scattered about on a pine wood floor, and a large green top pool table sat toward the back of the room.

Overhead can lighting and vintage-style pendant lights hung from the ceiling in bronze. There was a small stage with lights above and an empty mic standing solo. The jukebox in the corner was playing Leggs by ZZ Top! Jessica and I ordered two Sam Adams beers and took a seat at a table.

The patrons were male and female, most of them baby boomers with lifelong riding skills, some Gen Z's with designer leather apparel, and only a few looked like they were still part of the many well-known biker groups. It was a mixed bag here.

The server came by and brought out our beers.

"Here you are, two Sam Adams," she also placed some bar snacks down for us, a bowl of mixed nuts and pretzels.

"So what are a couple of cuties like you doing here? It doesn't seem like your scene."

"Looking for a friend," I responded.

"Well, you've come to the right place; there's always someone looking for someone. A husband, a boyfriend, a brother, a sister, a mother, or even a father, hell, we got drama in here every night, I should charge admission."

"This is your bar?" I asked her.

"Yup, the name's Lee." She put out her hand.

Lee seemed like a no-nonsense gal, maybe late 50s, with blondish-gray curly hair but still full of fight. With her Wrangler jeans, black Harley t-shirt, bright pink lipstick, and Candies' style women's wooden high heels, she seemed like a biker, Dolly Parton.

"I'm Nikki, and this is Jessica. So, how long have you owned the bar?"

"Oh, ever since my husband won it at a poker game, it's a long story, but he's dead, and now I run the place."

"I'm sorry about your husband. It's nice to see more women entrepreneurs."

"I think it's cool," Jessica commented.

"Oh, don't feel bad for me. Wyatt took care of me, and he smoked since he was 12 years old, so we knew it was come'n but God rest his sweet soul. Well, if you ladies need anything else, let me know."

"Thanks," we both smiled.

"So what do we do next?" Jessica asked me.

"I guess we could ask around."

"What do we ask? Hey, have you seen Freddie Santana?"

I snacked on the bar mix, and Jessica and I came up with a plan.

We decided to start a game of pool to get comfortable with the surroundings and then maybe strike up a conversation with the regulars. We finished our beers first. Then I racked up the balls at the pool table, and Jessica broke.

"Cool, I'm stripes." She cheered.

Jessica took her shot again, but she missed her five-ball. I scanned the green. My three-ball was close enough to the middle pocket, but it looked impossible without hitting Jessica's ball.

"50 bucks says you can't make that shot!"

An older man who looked like he drained the Botox factory stood by my center pocket.

He was dressed in black jeans and a very expensive leather jacket, which had probably never seen the open road; it was hanging open, with a black T-shirt, one with orange Harley Davidson flames on it underneath.

His black bike boots looked expensive and barely used.

Trendsetter huh!

He winked at me, holding that bill like he was waiting for a bull to charge at him.

If I had to guess, I think he's probably a surgeon at some fancy hospital. I noticed a gold, gleaming wedding band on his finger! Huh, married, he didn't score points with me! I had to get rid of this one and fast!

"I'm not interested in bets."

I told him, with a cold brush off.

I got ready to make my shot, and just when I was ready to take the turn, he then sat on the pool table and fanned out $200.00 bucks. He dragged it along my arm and winked at me.

"What if I sweeten the pot, little chica?"

I stopped what I was doing and stood up.

"Excuse me, what did you just say?"

Jessica's eyes loomed large; she slowly took a step back. My eyebrow arched high, and my hand was now on my hip, confronting him. Chica was ok when my friends said it endearingly, but when a womanizer used it as a pickup line, all I saw was red.

The jerk jumped off the table and tucked his money back in his pocket.

"I guess you're not interested in men."

"Yes, just not you!" I replied.

He whispered under his breath, "bitch."

"You should be more respectful with women."

I told him, standing in front of him, still holding the pool cue.

"Nikki, let's go!"

Jessica said, coming over to me and tugging my arm to put down the pool cue.

"He's not worth it."

I dropped the cue on the table and gave him a hard, evil eye stare. I had a small audience around watching us. The music was blaring in the background to Joan Jett's "I Don't Give a Dam about my bad reputation."

I agreed with her; the last thing I wanted was to get into a bar brawl with *this* guy.

"Listen to your girlfriend."

He sarcastically said and walked away. Just then, the front door opened, and a tall, pretty redhead spotted her husband and yelled, "Dennis, you lying SOB!"

She charged in and grabbed the guy who had just tried to make a bet with me while hitting on me and insulting me. Jessica and I stood watching.

"You said you were at a meeting with colleagues at Desert Surgical Center. Yet I find you here!"

Bingo, was I right?

Dennis was speechless; he replied, "Honey, I just wanted to stop and get a drink, that's all."

Next thing we know, a pretty brunette walked up to them.

"Dennis, you said you were a widow!"

"What!" The wife responded.

"Honey, she's lying. I never said that."

Dennis tried to brush off the brunette woman as he pandered to his wife.

"Yes, you did, you said that's why you still wear your ring to honor her death."

The brunette responded with her hands on her hips, very matter-of-fact.

Dennis shook his head; he was scared now!

The wife was at her boiling point by now; the look on her face said you are so dead!

"That's it, Dennis!"

The wife threw down the gauntlet!

The brunette pulled at Dennis's arm now.

"So does this mean we're not getting married, Dennis?"

Clueless that she was.

"No, it means you can have his cheating butt when I'm done taking every cent from him!"

She threw a right hook at Dennis.

"You'll hear from my lawyer!"

He almost fell over but recovered and put his hand to his face.

"Not the face, Kitty."

He said, rubbing the spot she punched.

"You can't hit him!"

The brunette took a swing at the wife and then missed.

The wife landed another punch and got her square in the jaw.

All of the people in the bar were watching, and some were getting excited by saying, "Hit her again!"

Jessica and I walked over to the bar while this was playing out.

A few people were recording this on their cell phones.

"Lee, I think you may need to call the cops; you have a situation here," I told her.

"Oh no! Not another girl-on-girl fight, that's the third one this week."

"Serves him right for what he's done, and not to mention he tried to pick up on us too," Jessica told Lee.

"He tried that stuff on you two, oh my word, Dennis has no shame, he's on his fourth marriage. Well, I reckon he's gonna pay for it."

Lee went behind the bar.

The two girls started again, and now the brunette grabbed the wife by the hair, dragging her, and they went fighting around the room.

The wife hit back but lost her balance, and then they both fell over some chairs, but they weren't done yet. The wife got the upper hand, took a beer bottle, and hit her over the head with it.

The gal went down, and Dennis ran over to her.

"I'm a doctor, call 911."

He yelled out.

The wife went for Dennis again; she must have been a former MMA fighter because she was kicking butt. Dennis went down next to his girlfriend, who was out cold. Then he got back up, staggering.

"That's enough, Kitty, I'm sorry."

"Oh, you'll be sorry."

She uppercut him in the gut.

He doubled over, and she pulled his hairpiece off.

Someone had called the cops, and they came in and broke up the fight. The wife sat down on a chair, and Lee brought her a shot of tequila.

"Here, Kitty, I thought you could use one."

"Thanks, Lee," she took one gulp, and down it went,

"Don't worry, I'll pay you for any damage I did, Lee."

"Thank you, Kitty and honey, those MMA classes you took are paying off. You looked like a pro."

"Thanks, Lee!" Kitty smiled; she looked satisfied.

Next, the EMTs arrived and gave Dennis's girlfriend smelling salts, and she woke up with a bolt!

They took her outside to the waiting ambulance, and Dennis accompanied her. No one pressed any charges, so the cops waved and smiled at Lee and ducked out and took off.

Everyone returned to their drinks and bar food; the pool table had some new players, and the jukebox played a softer tune.

Kitty took a seat, and Lee brought her a Bloody Mary.

Jessica and I went back to the bar.

"We should just ask Lee if anyone knows if Freddie was here, and if anyone would know, she would."

"I agree!" Jessica said.

Lee came back around the bar, starting the next order.

"Lee, I just had a question for you."

"Shoot, honey, what you wanna know?"

"By any chance, did Freddie Santana swing by here?"

She knew something, but she didn't want to say anything

I followed up with,

"His band, T-bone, Flick, Boss, and Parker, are worried about him, and so is Bobby, his manager. I promised T-Bone I would look around for him."

"Are you a private investigator?"

She asked, still a little hesitant to answer any questions.

"No, I'm a singer who owns a bar and restaurant."

She was moving something over in her mind; then she came out with it,

"I'll tell you what you sing me a song up there, and I'll tell ya what you wanna know."

"What do you want me to sing?"

I got up on the small stage, and Lee introduced me.

"All right, folks, tonight we have a local gal here, so be nice. Introducing Nikki Rodriguez."

All I had was background karaoke music; there's a first for everything, I thought.

I bolted out "Hit Me with Your Best Shot" by Pat Benatar.

I finished with a round of applause and requests for another song, so I sang another Pat Benatar song, "Treat Me Right."

I thanked everyone for their kind words. I even got a job offer to sing for a couple who are going to have their 50th anniversary coming up in August.

I sat down at the bar, and Lee had a fresh beer waiting for me

"It's on the house, honey."

I smiled, "Now, about that information."

"A promise is a promise." She responded.

She told me Freddie had come in yesterday, and he was keeping a low profile; he just wanted to hang out and relax; he wasn't off in a hurry, and he wasn't being kidnapped; he just wanted some free time. Lee said that Freddie was an old friend of hers from way back in the day when he first started out. He used to play at places like Axeles bar, and he missed the small stage.

She said he didn't tell her where he was going, but just that he would be back in a few days and had to explain to the guys in his band why he left.

"Honey, I didn't get too personal with him, so he didn't tell me any more than that, but I reckon he will come back when he is ready!"

"Thanks, Lee."

Jessica and I called it a night and headed back to Rancho Niguel.

Chapter 10

Grand Opening

Today was the big grand opening of the Youth Center. The finishing touches had been completed, and Sam and his crew had done a fantastic job. The ribbon cutting would begin at 5 pm today, with many residents in attendance. The staff, the mentors, the board, and kids, parents, and even a donor or two. When I got home from the biker bar last night, Sara was true to her word; she was snuggled up with blankets and asleep on the sofa, with the TV still on.

A Netflix series about the Addams family is what it looked like, called Wednesday. It looked very entertaining, and I would have to check it out. I turned off the TV and went to bed.

This morning, she was up early and already making breakfast. She is so much like Matt, the early riser, and always helpful.

I showered, brushed my teeth, and dressed. I walked to the kitchen and poured myself a cup of French press coffee.

"Late night?"

Sara asked, serving up some pancakes with syrup.

"My friend Jessica and I went to check out a lead on a case I'm independently working on."

"Matt always tells me about your cases; he said you're like a detective, like the Charlie's Angels type. So tell me, what are you working on?"

I filled her in on the case of the missing rock star Freddie Santana. I also told her about my brush with death, the nail gun incident, and the damage to the gym at the Youth Center.

"Nikki, someone is trying to kill you!"

"I know, but Paul doesn't have much to go on. The only fingerprints on the nail gun were Sam's, the contractor, and two of his employees. They are all clean, with no criminal records, and I don't know them that well enough to make enemies."

"You said the gym floor was vandalized, and Matt told me the restaurant Kendle's, where you work, was vandalized back in December. Do you think they both have to do with you?"

"Yes, I do, and I have an idea who it might be, but I don't have any proof."

"Who do you think it is?"

"It's just a theory, but I think it's Paul's ex-girlfriend Stacie Mc. Daniels!"

"Tell me more."

I gave Sara my theory about Stacie, right down to the way she constantly scowls at me and her fake smile with Paul and her brother Matt."

"Nikki, do you think she would go through all of this over a guy?"

"Do you remember what happened to your brother with that woman Trixie last summer?"

"Oh yeah, Mom was so worried about Matt, she's been bugging him to move to Vegas or Thousand Oaks with my brothers. He was very clear that he is perfectly happy here in Rancho Niguel. Not to mention, she said she would like to see my brother get married already. He needs to settle down! Ugg, she is always off nagging at one of us!"

I chuckled at her response, "Your brother is going to do what he wants to do, and nothing will change that."

"Yeah, but she married the other two of my brothers off, and she's on a mission!"

"Speaking of your family, what are you going to do?"

"You can drop me off at Matt's house tomorrow morning, but I want to stay in Rancho Niguel. Help me, Nikki?"

"Let's see what we can work out."

I told Sara I had to be at the Youth Center grand opening at five, and if she wanted to hang out here, that would be fine.

She said she would be at Violet's house but would be home early.
On my way out, I saw Craig coming from his place. He jumped
down off the last step and called me out.

"Nikki, I'm glad I caught up with you."

He was carrying a small moving box with the SEES candy emblem
on it.

Oh man, not again! What is the hellish product he's going to get
me for today? I should just hand him my wallet and tell him to go
ahead and rip me off!

He was happy and full of sunshine,

"So my niece is selling SEES chocolates for her fundraiser. I told
her you love to support kids and that you would be a great
customer."

"Craig, I'm on my way out right now."

He opened the box and showed me five dozen candy bars, milk
chocolate with or without nuts, wrapped in Valentine's Day paper.
20 of the famous suckers in butterscotch and chocolate, and about
10 chocolate hearts in a clear bag with red and pink hearts on them.

"I'll take two chocolate bars."

"Nikki, you can do better than that!" He said.

I rolled my eyes. "Ok, three bars."

He made a face that showed his disappointment.

Just then, a little girl of seven or eight came up right beside Craig.

"Uncle Craig, is this Nikki? Did she buy the whole box like you said she would!"

The little girl chimed with enthusiasm and a big smile across her face.

I looked at Craig, and he smiled slightly and shrugged his shoulders

"Thank you, Ms. Nikki, you're just as nice as Uncle Craig said you were."

I didn't have the heart to deny her the happiness written across her little face, her cute little brown braids with red ribbons on them, and her denim jumper overalls. She was adorable.

"Of course, I bought the whole box, sweetie. I'm happy to help."
I smiled.

She hugged me and thanked me again. Craig handed me the box, and I asked him how much I owed him.

"Just leave me a check for..." He fished out a form in the box with the total for the candy plus sales tax, "It comes up to $357.35, Nikki."

I silently gritted my teeth, but wrote him a check, I gave it to him, and I took the box from him.

The little girl said thank you again, and she ran upstairs.

"Wait until Auntie Kiana hears this, it's so cool!"

When she was out of earshot, I told Craig

"You owe me!"

He nodded and didn't say anything, just walked back upstairs.

I took the box of chocolates to my place and left them on the table.

I ran to the bug once again, now running late.

When I arrived at the Youth Center, I spotted Paul's Army green

truck in the parking lot, and Matt's Red truck was there as well.

The community board members were milling about and

everyone was lining up for the ribbon-cutting.

"Oh, good, you're here." Ms. Mayor said as I took my place at the

entrance. "I apologize for being late. I had a prior engagement that

slightly went over."

"That's ok, let's get this going."

Her smile was tenfold; she looked a little psychotic, like she was

on a heavy dose of meds.

She handed me some very large, makeshift scissors, and the press

that was here lined up to get their photos.

I spotted Paul sitting next to Stacie. He waved at me and smiled.

Stacie glared! People gathered around now to eagerly await the

ribbon-cutting. Mayor CJ took a microphone and introduced me

and the Youth Center.

"Thank you, everyone, for coming today. I am glad to invite you to

the new Rancho Niguel Youth Center. Thank you to our donors and

supporters for financing this facility. We are so grateful.

Now, Ms. Rodriguez, if you will do the honors."

I placed my black clutch purse under my arm; it matched my black pantsuit, which I wore with a white silk sleeveless blouse. I cut the red ribbon, and now white balloons fell from above us. Everyone clapped and cheered. I shook the mayor's hand and smiled for the cameras; then, we opened the front doors for the community. Everyone walked through the entrance with big smiles on their faces, and energetic youngsters tugged at the arms of their parents as they eagerly went inside the building.

Matt tapped me on the shoulder, "Hey Nikki, you look nice."

"Thank you, Matt."

"So, what do you think of this place?"

I asked him.

"It looks really good, I think it's going to help our community a lot! You did a fabulous job, lady."

He smiled, giving me props for my hard work.

"Nikki,"

Paul walked up to us.

"Hi,"

Paul kissed my cheek and stood close to me. "Matt, how's it going?"

"Great," he said, putting some distance between Paul and me.

Stacie walked up to us. She didn't acknowledge me as usual but just went directly to Paul.

"I was going to give you a tour, Paul."

She told him.

She slipped her arm in the crook of his arm and attempted to pull him away. The look on my face said it all: *you are not taking my man anywhere!*

Paul didn't move and kindly told her,

"Matt hasn't had a chance to see the place. I think you should give him a tour."

Stacie, although disappointed, quickly recovered. She unhooked her arm from Paul and turned her attention to Matt. I know Matt saw the look I gave Stacie; it was impossible to miss.

"Captain Stevens, would you like a tour?"

"Of course, that would be nice, Stacie."

She slithered over to Matt and led him down toward the classrooms.

"So, is there anything new about my attacker?"

I asked Paul, skipping over the Stacie incident.

"I found some shoe prints out back; I had crime scene take a mold of them, we'll see where it leads,"

We toured the classrooms with parents and kids, many of them chatting with some instructors and volunteers. Others were busy sampling some of the treats here, especially at the frozen yogurt counter that we brought in at the snack stand.

"What department did they put you in, here at the youth center?" I asked Paul as we circled.

"Stacie said she put me in the aquatic and lifesaving area. I'll be teaching some intermediate and advanced swim classes for kids, one for all ages, *Just Say No To Drugs,* and one *Teen Crime class."*

"That's awesome! Matt told me they placed him in *CPR training* and *Fire Safety* for all ages, and he's coaching *little league baseball for* ages 5-7!" I said as we made our way to the gym for the recital.

We took a seat on the new bleachers along with everyone else. Stacie and Matt walked to us and took seats right next to us, with Stacie on one side and Paul and me on the other side. Matt sat next to me. The show began with two bands, one from West Rancho Niguel High and one from Rancho Niguel High School; they played "Jessie's Girl" by Rick Springfield.

Dancers twirled about the gym floor, and cheerleaders danced with their pom poms as well.

Everyone clapped when they were done, and the mayor came back to her mic.

"Everyone, please give another round of applause for these kids; they were wonderful!"

The crowd showed their appreciation for the youngster's performance. Clapping and cheering for them.

"Next, we have a performance by Nikki Rodriguez."

I handed my clutch bag to Paul to hold for me, and I walked up to the mic in my black stilettos. The band played my intro to the song "Under Pressure" By Queen and David Bowie, two awesome rock artists and two of my favs.

The high school bands were stellar on the drums, horns, and violins, along with two guitar players, and the choir sang the David Bowie part of the song as my duet partners. We rocked! The ending of the song brought in the entire band playing and bringing the house down. The dancers did their routine to the song, and when we ended, we got a standing ovation. More balloons fell from the ceiling, and streamers were shot out of streamer canons. It felt like a concert from the Mission at Rancho Niguel. Everyone cheered, and I high-fived both of my guitarists.

We all took our bows, and Paul and Matt cheered and whistled.

The mayor was ecstatic; she came to us with all of her energy.

"Wow! Was that a show? I'm so proud of all of you."

She clapped.

The audience sent whistles and cheers.

The only one not smiling and celebrating was Stacie Mc. Daniels!

Chapter 11

Poor Little Bug

After the performance, the grand opening ended, and now everyone said goodbyes and walked to their cars. A small line of vehicles exiting had caused a bit of traffic to form. Paul, Matt, and I walked to my car. The Mayor had left in her limo, and Stacie was AWOL. Hmm, strange! I thought for sure she would be hanging all over Paul right about now, but she had left right after my song.

I stopped in front of my car to unlock my door when I saw the word DIE scratched into the side of my car; the red paint peeled away from the metal underneath it. "What the heck?"

Paul and Matt stared in shock.

"Nikki, I can't believe someone did this to your car!"

Matt said in awe.

"Man, this is getting out of hand," Paul said. He called it in, and soon, he was investigating my car and the bitter scene before me.

"This sucks!" I said, holding back my anger.

Matt put an arm around me, "I'm so sorry, darlin'."

"It can be fixed," I replied.

Paul walked over, and Matt released me.

"I'm more concerned with the message."

In Paul's gloved hand was a note.

"This was under the wipers."

It read:

This time, it's your car

Next time, it will be you!

"I don't know who is doing this."

Paul said out loud with frustration.

I opened my door and tried to start my car, but nothing happened.

"Nikki, pop the hood," Paul asked. He and Matt stood in front of the car waiting.

I pulled the handle under the steering wheel, but nothing happened.

"It's not working,"

I yelled out.

"It looks like someone pried it open."

Paul raised the hood and turned on his small flashlight.

"Uh, Nikki, I think your car needs to be towed, it's not going to start,"

Matt said.

Paul beckoned me over.

I walked around to see what the fuss was!

They were right,

I would have to have my car towed. The engine was melted by acid! Steam was now rising from the engine high into the midnight sky.

After forensics had arrived and gathered their evidence, Paul drove me home.

Matt had left a few minutes earlier and insisted that Paul provide me with police protection, with Diaz just as he had before. Paul said he would do everything in his power to keep me safe.

I sent a text to Sara's burner phone that she purchased for her time away from home to let her know Paul was driving me back; I told her to hang out in my room with the door closed.

I hadn't told Paul or anyone else that Sara was staying with me. She said she would be on her social media with her Bluetooth earbuds.

In the car, I decided I would tell Paul that I had the suspicion Stacie was behind all of this. I knew he would be defensive, but he had to be thinking the same thing, right?

I approached the conversation delicately; only I'm not that delicate!

"Paul, I have to tell you something you might not want to hear. I think I know who is trying to kill me."

"Yeah, who do you think is behind this?"

His face filled with concern and eagerness to know who was the mystery assailant.

"It's Stacie!" I blurted out.

Paul chuckled in surprise.

"Wait, are you serious?"

My face never had a more serious look than it did right now.

"You don't believe me?"

"I think that's a long shot. Stacie doesn't even know you that well."

My nerve was touched, and now I had unleashed some of my frustration.

"You're kidding! Haven't you seen the way she looks at me? It's like the woman is ready to tear me up into little pieces!"

"I think you're wrong. She's focused on her job. It's been a little hard taking orders from the mayor; she's a bit overwhelming, but Stacie has been a trooper. She has a demanding job with a lot of responsibilities."

Shut my mouth and slap me twice. Was he for real?

I was shocked, but now it all made sense to me; I just had been refusing to see it. He still had feelings for Stacie, and I was out here all alone; he wouldn't take it well when it turned out to be Stacie behind this. Would he try to protect her?

Would he try to steer the blame away from her?

"Look, I know what you're thinking, Nikki, it's not that I'm on her side; I'm looking at this from a police point of view, and there isn't any evidence that she has any blame here."

"Who else would do this? I don't have any enemies." I responded with a chill in my tone.

We arrived in front of my condo, and he put the car in park and turned to me.

"Nikki, I'll tell you what, I will find out the truth, but you have to promise me that you will trust me."

I focused my attention on the trees outside while my thoughts spun a million miles a minute about the fact that Paul was now biased. He wouldn't listen to me!

He turned the car off and opened his door.

He came around and opened the door for me, and I exited. We walked to my front door, with silence between us.

Paul looked around, checking the courtyard around us, while I unlocked the door.

We went inside, and he locked my deadbolt.

I put my coat in the coat closet and walked to the kitchen.

I pulled a bottle of red wine from the wine rack on the kitchen wall.

I popped it open and poured a glass for myself.

I took a drink and let the sweet chocolate, berry flavor of the 2020 vintage reach my taste buds and enjoyed the rush of flavor.

I set down my glass, took a deep breath, and exhaled.

Paul walked over to me and put his hand around my waist. His forehead leaned to mine, and he whispered to me.

"Nikki, I'm going to find the truth, and whatever it is, I'll accept it, but if it's not what you expected, will you accept it?"

He was being a detective now and doing all that he could to convince me he would be impartial and that he would be the detective I knew he was.

He closed his eyes and drank in the warmth of my arms at his sides, my lips coming to his now.

"Paul Anderson, I trust you."

He kissed me, and we embraced one another, and I knew he still loved me.

Chapter 12

I need some Wheels

I made a cup of French press coffee, took my cup out on the patio, and sat in the warm sunshine. Spring was on its way. Our winter was very mild, not too cold, not too hot. A light breeze blew by and gave my potted red pansies and yellow marigolds a shake. Finally, my gardening skills have improved, and I have healthy plants and flowers now.

The patio slider opened, and Sara came out and sat next to me.

"Good morning, did you sleep well?"

I asked her.

"Your bed is very comfortable," Sara replied with a cup of coffee in her hand and still in her jammies. Last night, after Paul left, Sara had fallen asleep in my bed, so I covered her with my comforter, and I took a pillow and a blanket out to the sofa. I didn't have the heart to wake her, so I camped out on the couch.

"Well, you looked so comfortable, I didn't want to wake you."

"Thanks, I was exhausted. Jagger and I went hiking on the Mt. Wilson trail yesterday, and after that, we went with Violet to get some dinner and play a round of miniature golf. By the time they dropped me off, I was ready for a bath and bed."

"So I know that I'm supposed to drop you off at your brother's, but we have a slight problem."

I told her about the grand opening at the Youth Center and then the death of my bug.

"No way, Nikki, so what are you going to do now?"

"I need a new car!"

Sara and I took an Uber to the Volkswagen mechanic on Horseshoe Dr.

We got out and then walked into the open garage.

The bug sadly sat there defeated.

The car had been towed here early this morning by the police department after they fingerprinted it and searched it for any clues. I knew there wouldn't be any; the person doing this had covered their tracks fairly well.

A man in a blue work jumpsuit with a name tag that read *Buck* walked up to us.

"Can I help you?" He asked, wiping his greased hands with a yellow rag.

"Yes, that's my bug there. Any word yet on whether or not it's fixable?"

"Oh man, well, this one is a first for us!"

He scratched his head in amazement.

"We've never seen anything like this before. I hate to tell you, but it's not fixable."

He told us.

"The acid dripped all over the motor and the radiator."

With his hands on his hips, he made his most professional estimate.

"We can pull everything out of it and replace the motor, radiator, vacuum lines, electronics, and so forth, but you're looking at at least $18k, including parts and labor, and that's only if we don't have to replace the dashboard, the damage might have gone to the wheel wells and brakes.

It's a total loss. I can offer you $5 grand for the parts; most likely, I can use it for that. Your interior seems fine, and the windows, car doors, and the back of the vehicle are salvageable."

I knew it before he even had to say anything; it was totaled!

"Well, I guess I'll take the five grand."

Sara and I caught a Lyft, and we were dropped off at Rancho Car Rentals. We walked in; we were the only ones there at 10:30 am.

The dude behind the counter was typing a million miles a minute, studious in his work. He looked up as we arrived at his counter.

"Hello, how may I assist you today? My name is Jed."

His 200-watt smile bordering on scary and deranged!

"Good morning, I need a rental for a few days, maybe three or four."

"Are you new in town, business or pleasure, did you have a breakdown, or are you a local?" His voice took on a whine and a high pitch from his fast questions.

"My car is totaled, so I need a rental until I can purchase a new one."

"Oh, my gawd! I'm soooo sorry, what happened? Please tell me?" He put his hands under his chin, waiting for the gossip to hit my lips. Sara took a few steps back with eyebrows raised.

We exchanged a quick look that said oh my!

"The story is that someone poured acid on my car!"

"Oh my Gawd, seriously, wow, it's so scary, like Glen Close Fatal Attraction kind of creepy. Are you ok?"

He asked.

"Yes, the police are taking care of everything, so what about that car?"

"Oh, you poor thing, well, let me see what I have for you."

He typed away on his keyboard fast, the keys clicking away with his speed.

"Ok, ok, I do have one green minivan and two Jeep Wranglers, one in white and one in bright yellow."

"I'll take the white Jeep."

"Great choice, we just got this one in. It's brand new, and you're the first person to rent it, so it's Tre' chic. Just make sure no one gives you another acid trip, babe, ok."

He typed away, and two seconds later, I handed over my credit card, signed some forms, and then we were done.

"Ok, Nikki, here are the key fobs, it's parked right outside for you, girl, and just take care, ok."

I smiled.

"Thank you, Jed."

Sara and I got into the Jeep, and we were off. She had promised to go to Matt's house this afternoon and put an end to her runaway trip. This morning, before we left for the mechanics, she called her brother and told him she would go to his place. Matt told her to come to the station because he would be at work today.

She agreed and said she would be by later this afternoon.

Sara wanted to hang out with me for a few hours more. We headed to Kendle's, Tito and Daisy were back from their honeymoon, and I had to fill them in on everything that was going on.

Paul had texted me as we pulled into my parking stall.

"Hi Nikki, just FYI,

No prints were found in the bug other than

yours and mine and Roxi's.

We looked at the cameras from the youth center, and all that I

could see was an assailant

dressed in a mask with a black hoodie

And baggy jeans. Not sure if it's a

man or a woman.

I'm sending Diaz to you

stay alert, please."

I responded.

"Thanks for your hard work

I appreciate it. I'm at Kendle's

I'll be here most of the day,

just have Diaz come to the

kitchen door and up the stairs to my office."

He responded.

"How about dinner this evening?"

"Sure, come by tonight, and we can get some dinner!"

"Ok, Nikki, see you then."

Sara had walked into Kendle's and was waiting patiently in the

lobby by the hostess desk.

I walked in and was greeted by Daisy

"Nikki," she hugged me.

"Oh, Daisy, how was your trip to Catalina Island?"

"We had such a great time, Nikki, it was wonderful."

"Daisy, let me introduce you to Sara, Matt's younger sister."

They shook hands and said nice to meet you.

"I have so much to tell you, Daisy, you won't believe what is going on right now!"

"Uh oh, I leave you for a week and a half, and you have new drama." She said.

"Drama isn't the word, come on, I'll fill you guys in."

We walked to the bar, where Tito was setting up some new bottles of tequila.

"Hey, boss, we missed you!"

Tito came around the bar and gave me a big bear hug.

"I missed you guys, too!"

"Hey Tito, Nikki has some stuff going on!"

Daisy called out.

"We leave for a week and a half, and you have stuff going on?"

Tito asked. Surprised and worried in one expression on his face, he did the eyebrow raise thing and made me and Sara giggle.

I flipped my hair and said, "Oh boy, where do I start..."

Chapter 13

Sara Smiles

I briefed Tito and Daisy on everything from Sara running away to the jam with Freddie Santana, to the nail gun incident, the death of the bug, and the fact that someone out there still wants my head on a platter.

Daisy was shocked! She tsk'd and said,

"Wow, all of this drama in Rancho Niguel."

"Never a dull moment here."

Tito said.

We were upstairs in my office, and I had let Sara stay in the kitchen where Chef Stark was showing her how to make chocolate frosting.

"Well, Nikki, I will say this: I think you love the kid. Not many people would go to these lengths to help her out and to keep this from Matt."

Tito responded.

"Yeah, well, we were all young at one time. I get it: she misses her friends, and she wants to stay here where she feels comfortable, but she's going to her brothers' tonight.

After that, she's going to make her plea to stay here and live with Matt. I mean, he has all of that room in that big house, and Sara can go back to her old school and maybe get a part-time job; she has options."

"She's lucky she has you, Nikki, but man, that business of Freddie Santana walking out on his band, have you heard any more about where he is?"

Daisy asked.

"Nope, the last place he was at was that bar, Axels, I guess he'll be back when he's ready."

We went back downstairs, and Tito and Daisy went back to work, and I went to find Sara.

Diaz was hanging out in the kitchen, asking about me.

"There she is!"

Diaz said, walking up to me. Looking ever the calm and cool cop that he is. His Ray Ban aviators resting on top of his head. He was casual in a dark suit with no tie.

"I guess you're my shadow again, huh?"

"De Ja Vu, right! Don't worry, Nikki, we're going to catch this person."

"I can't wait! Come on, I'll introduce you."

Chef Stark had Sara icing the cakes, two of them to be exact, laid out on the kitchen counter.

She had a white apron on, a hair net, and food prep gloves. With the icing spatula in her hand, she meticulously worked to create a smooth array of waves over the top of the cake.

"Excellent, Sara, you're a natural, are you sure you never did this before?"

Chef Stark asked her.

"Nope, first time."

Sara smiled.

"Hey, that looks great. Do you want a job here?" I asked.

"Maybe." She smiled.

When she finished her cakes, she took off her apron, gloves, and hair net. "That was cool, thank you for teaching me, Chef."

"You're welcome, Sara."

"I need to steal Sara away right now, chef; she's going to go to her brother's house."

"Hey, well, come back another day, and I can teach you how to make pasta A La California. It's one of our most popular dishes."

"I will, thanks, dude."

I introduced her to Lt. Diaz. They shook hands, and she asked him, "You look like that guy on TV, the hot guy, what's his name, cute Latino dude, um, oh what's his name, Mario Lopez." She snapped her fingers, hitting the answer she was looking for.

Diaz blushed, "I've had people tell me that before."

"So, Nikki, is there anything I should know about?"

"Jay Diaz is going to be my bodyguard for a few days."

"Oh, ok!"

We all went up to my office, and Sara had a seat on the sofa. Diaz stood by the door.

"So, do you run this place? Matt never mentioned it."

"I own this place with my stepdad; we're business partners."

"Wow, that's cool!"

"I don't tell everyone; the only ones that know are my staff, and Tito, Daisy, Paul, Jessica, Roxi, Craig, Martin, and Oliver. Oh yeah, and Diaz."

"Ok, got any other businesses?"

"A real estate office and my stepdad and some of his business partners financed the new Rancho Niguel Youth Center."

"Man, Nikki, you're rolling in everything." She smiled.

"Now, what are we going to do about getting you back to your brother?"

Sara frowned.

"I guess I'd better contact him!"

At 6 pm, Sara sent Matt a text.

"Hey, big bro, I'm heading over to the firehouse. I should be there in 20 minutes."

He responded

"Sara, I'll be inside my office."

Next, I sent a text to Matt.

Hi, just wondering if you heard from Sara?"

He texted back.

"She's on her way here; my folks came in late last night. That spare room came in handy. If you hear fireworks, it's just my family arguing. Lol"

"I had an idea about Sara; I think she should stay and live with you. She only has two years left of school, and I bet it would be good to have family so close. You're an excellent role model, and your parents want her to be happy. I think it could work."

He responded with,

"That's an idea; I'll pitch it to my parents and see what they say. Thanks, Nikki."

"Anytime, Matt."

"Sara, Matt just said your folks are already here, so now it's show time. Try to convince them to let you stay here. I already gave Matt the idea. He thought it was a good one."

"Thanks, Nikki." Sara smiled.

We pulled up to the fire station a block before so that Matt wouldn't see me drop Sara off. Diaz sat in the back seat and stayed silent.

"Ok, Nikki, wish me luck!"

"Good luck, sweetie. Call me later and tell me what happened."

"Ok." She said, sounding hopeful. She took a deep breath and got out of the jeep.

I waited until I saw her go inside, and then Diaz jumped in the front seat, and we drove off.

Later that day, Paul came by Kendle's and relieved Diaz from his shift.

When we were alone, he kissed me passionately and then asked me "So, what do you feel like having for dinner?"

"There's a cool fondue restaurant that just opened."

We arrived at DIP, the new romantic fondue restaurant; the room was dimmed. The seating was Moroccan style, with pillows and short tables. Red hearts and cupids were everywhere; we were greeted by a hostess dressed in a white dress with angel wings attached to her back. Wow, why didn't I think of that?

We were seated at a table in the corner; we ordered the Cupid's Feast. It came with chunks of steak, chicken, shrimp, raw veggies of broccoli, carrots, and green beans. Cubes of sourdough and herbed croutons. I ordered a glass of red wine, and Paul ordered a beer.

We pushed small talk and avoided discussing work; we needed boyfriend and girlfriend time.

"The steak is amazing!" I said, taking a piece and dipping it in oozing, melted white cheddar.

"Save room for dessert," Paul said, dipping a piece of shrimp in melted white cheddar cheese.

I told him about Sara being reunited with her folks and about her staying at Matt's to finish high school.

He thought it was a good idea, too!

"It must be hard for Sara. All of her friends are back here, and with social media, she had to be feeling left out. Now, it's not just the thought of missing your friends, it's actually watching them have a good time without you. What kids go through today is a lot different from when we were teens."

Paul said with concern.

"I agree, Paul. I hope everything works out for her."

I told him.

When we finished our chocolate fondue with cubes of angel food cake, strawberries, and marshmallows, we walked back to Kendle's.

Paul followed me back to my place.

"So, how do you like driving the Jeep?"

Paul asked me.

"I like it; I might buy one."

We went inside; it was a little chilly. I flipped on the fireplace, and we sat on the sofa.

I got a text message from Matt.

"Sara is going to stay with me while she goes to school; my parents couldn't bear to see her unhappy anymore. Looks like we found a solution to one of my empty rooms.

Thank you, Nikki,"

"Good news, Paul, Sara is smiling now."

Chapter 14

Someone is Lying

After all of the fiasco of events, from the grand opening to my car being murdered to Sara coming back home, I finally had a moment to think about something. I had watched the local news and even read the local paper, and I had yet to see an article penned by my good buddy Flame about the new Youth Center.

I thought it was odd because I hadn't seen Flame at the grand opening, so what happened?

I decided to send Flame a text message and ask him if he wanted to grab a coffee or a late lunch tomorrow.

"Hi, buddy,

Nikki here, just wondering if you wanted to get together since you are in town this week. Let me know."

He replied after five minutes

"Hi, Nikki,

Good to hear from you, sorry I can't get together, but I'm in Europe doing a story on the royals. I will be here in London for the next couple of weeks. Maybe when I get back to the States, we can get together. You should come to New York, it's amazing!"

I was stunned. Didn't he have a family thing that he was coming to California for?

"Flame, I was told you were going to be here for a family event and that you would be interviewing the mayor about the new community youth center. Am I wrong?"

"Wow! No one told me about this! My family is in Idaho visiting some extended family. Someone gave you an earful."

"The mayor's office didn't try to contact you?"

"No!"

"Something stinks here, Flame. And I'm going to find out!"

"Nikki, you're back on a case, I take it, huh?"

"You have no idea."

"Nikki, just watch your back; it seems like there is trouble in Rancho Niguel for you again."

"Flame, you are correct!"

After our fifteen-minute conversation, I told Flame a little bit about what was happening here. He was surprised and told me that if I needed any help, just give him a ring. I kept that in my back pocket and thanked him for his help.

So my mind went into full-blown detective mode: Who gave the wrong information? Was it Stacie? Did she lie just to appease the mayor? Was it the mayor? Did she lie just to give herself more importance? Someone was lying, and now I needed to find out who and why.

My first order of business today would be to find out who was lying. I decided first to speak to Stacie.

I had to close Kendle's this evening, so I had time now during the day to do some investigating. I have suspected Stacie this whole time of being behind the incidents at the Youth Center and the damage to my car. Now, I needed proof to nail her for the crimes. I drove down to the city hall building located next to the cultural arts and library, across from the mall.

Diaz waited right outside the building for me. Walking into the building, I had a De Ja Vu of the last time I was here; it was to come and see the former mayor's wife and gather clues to solve the murder of my neighbor, Chanel O'Conner. The offices looked exactly as they had one year ago, the gleaming wood floors and calm sage walls, and the lemon polish smell that wafted throughout the room.

Marge, my good old pal. Sat at her desk today. She was dressed in a light blue and cream-flowing dress. Her favorite fabric being light linen. Her curly hair, a little longer now, was set in a scarf-like headband with a tie-dye design. Large light blue hoop earrings dangled from her earlobes, and her gold-rimmed glasses made her light blue eyes brighter.

"Hello, Marge, how are you?"

"Oh, Nikki, sweetie, how are you?" She came around the desk and gave me a big hug.

"You're looking fantastic today. Besides, I haven't seen you since Christmas." She told me.

We sat down and began our conversation with more detail.

"Oh, thank you. We need to catch up."

"We sure do, you know what, you should come to our bridge party; we have one twice a month, and you know everyone there. We are having our next one in April because a few of us are going to San Diego for a week-long vacation. Keep your calendar open for April 17."

"Ok, I will. I have a quick question: do you think it would be possible to speak with Stacie Mc. Daniels?"

"Oh, um, well, she's not here at the moment. Mayor CJ has her running some errands, but she should be back by 3:30."

"Ok, I guess I can come back around that time."

I checked my watch, and it read 11:45 am.

"Are, are you friends with her?"

Marge asked with some hesitation about asking me this.

"No! I have to speak with her."

"I see," Marge replied. She knew what was going on.

"I hope you'll forgive my prying, but does it have to do with Det. Anderson?"

"What have you heard, Marge?"

I smiled slightly.

"Oh, dear, let me speak freely on that one. Your beau has been here a few times to see the Mayor, and that Stacie is stuck on him. She follows him around, smiling and flirting and pretending to be the damsel in distress. Uggg, it's nauseating."

She waved her arm as if she were swatting a fly.

"I know she wants him back, and I have to say I'm worried."

"Oh, Nikki, he has been the gentleman that you love, trust me, he has only shown her kindness, that's all, if anything, he seems like he's always running away from her."

"That's good to know."

"I'll tell you, though, I get the feeling she is up to something. She acts so professionally in front of the mayor, but when the mayor isn't around, she tries to boss everyone around and starts ordering me to get her lunch and to do this and that. I seriously thought of putting in my retirement papers early, and I only have a year and a half left."

"Do you think she is trying to sabotage the mayor?"

"I think she wants to be mayor. But you didn't hear that from me."

Marge had whispered, but looked very uneasy when she told me this.

I had the feeling that my spidey senses were right on track. Stacie was up to something, and it wasn't good!"

"Nikki, if you need me to keep an ear and an eye open, I can do that," Marge told me, winking.

This was what I needed: someone on the inside to give me the information about what was going on here.

"Marge, I'm going to take you up on that."

Chapter 15

Hello Freddie

After going to the mayor's office, Marge and I devised a plan to watch Stacie and find out if we could get any proof for Paul that she was the one terrorizing me. My next assignment was...

My phone rang, and the name read MATT.

"Hi, Matt,"

"Hi, Nikki, I just wanted to thank you for all of your help trying to find Sara."

"It was no problem, really, I'm glad she is safe and sound."

"So Sara wanted to see you, and we were wondering if you had any dinner plans this evening?"

Wow! Did he just catch me off guard? I had about a million things to do. Tomorrow is Valentine's Day, and the big dinner at Kendle's. From 11 am to midnight, I was going to be there, and I was hoping to go to bed early tonight. I guess it couldn't hurt. I did have to keep up the pretense that I hadn't seen Sara in a few years. Otherwise, I would lead Matt to suspect something was off.

"I would love to see Sara. Can we make it an early dinner? I have to be at work all day tomorrow! I'd like to turn in early this evening."

"Of course, we can make it for 5:30 pm, how does that sound?"

"Ok, I can do that!"

"How about we meet at Snyder's Sports, Games, and Social."

"Sounds like fun, Matt, I'll be there."

"See you then,"

I headed back to Kendle's to get some work done for tomorrow. Just as I sat at my desk, my phone rang. It was from Axels bar.

"Hello."

"Nikki, it's Freddie. Can I meet you somewhere? I have a favor to ask you."

An hour later, Freddie came in through the back entrance of Kendle's and walked up the stairs to my office. Diaz nodded at him to enter. Freddie looked surprised to see my armed guard at my door.

"Freddie, it's good to see you again. Are you ok?"

He hugged me.

"No, that's why I'm here."

"Let's sit down." I ushered us over to the small sofa in the small lobby area.

"Would you like anything to drink?"

"No, thanks. You have armed security here?"

"Someone is trying to kill me."

"Oh, Nikki, that's terrible. Why would someone want to do that?" He looked worried.

"That's the big question."

"I guess you have your hands full; maybe this wasn't such a good idea."

"No, Freddie, how can I help?" I assured him

He looked a little reluctant but then said,

 "I just wanted to ask you to help me find some information on my manager, Bobby; I think he's stealing money from the band!"

The shock on my face said it all.

 "Really, what makes you think that he is stealing?"

"Inconsistencies!"

"Do you have any proof?"

"That's where you come in."

"Ok, what do you need?"

"I hear you know a lot of cops." He looked over at Diaz.

Freddie and I had a conference call with Paul about some surveillance on Bobby. We explained all of the details of the plan to get Bobby to fess up to the money he had been taking from the band. Money from gigs, endorsements, and local appearances. There were also some inconsistencies with the fan club accounting as well. Paul put us in touch with a buddy of his with the FBI white-collar crime division.

We needed help to find the trail of embezzlement that Bobby had allegedly committed! Freddie left after we hashed out the covert operation of this mission; he was meeting his band to have a long and overdue conversation with them. It was 4:45 pm, Diaz and I went downstairs, and Paul came by to relieve him.

"Say hi to Lindsey for me."

"I will, Nikki."

Within 15 minutes, Roxy walked into the kitchen from the back entrance, mascara streaming down her face.

"Can you believe he dumped me the day before Valentine's Day!"

Chapter 16

Dinner Anyone

My plans for the evening were completely hijacked! I had to help Roxy with her breakup; she didn't want to be alone tonight. Paul was expecting an evening just with the two of us, and my dinner with Matt and Sara included Matt's visiting parents. Could this night get any more weird?

I tried to tell Paul to go home and get some rest, and I would just take Roxy to my dinner. Paul wasn't having any of it, and in reality, I think he wanted to make sure my time with Matt was limited.

"If it's all right, I'd like to tag along, Nikki."

I called Matt to try to cancel our dinner, but no such luck.

"Matt, I need to cancel our dinner tonight. Roxy broke up with her boyfriend, and Paul had plans for us this evening. I'm so sorry, can we take a rain check for the day after Valentine's Day?"

"My mom and dad are leaving tomorrow to go back to Vegas. They have an early flight, and they wanted to see you, too! Invite Paul, and Roxy is always welcome, Sara has invited a friend of hers, the more the merrier, right?"

He was trying to convince me.

"I ... uh... Ok, I guess if it's no trouble." I said, stumbling out my sentence.

"Not at all, I'll call ahead and add two more places. See you in an hour."

"Ok." I hung up the phone and felt my stomach growl. Hunger pains? No! Stress pains!

Paul drove us over to Snyder's Sports, Games, and Social. It's been here a few years, but I haven't had a chance to dine here. The place is a restaurant with games, ping pong, shuffleboard, board games, a giant Twister game, a coin-operated arcade of pinball, a bowling alley, and sports of all types on the many TVs here; they have karaoke and ski ball lanes too. The menu is your basic burgers, sandwiches, salads, cool appetizers, brews, a vintage soda fountain, and an ice cream parlor. When we walked in, the music was blaring, playing "Miss You" by The Rolling Stones. The lobby was crowded with customers waiting for their names to be called to get a table. Our reservations were at 5:30, and we were five minutes late. The receptionist greeted us at the check-in desk. "Hi, we have a 5:30 reservation under Stevens."

"Oh yes, they are already seated. I'll take you to them."

We followed the hostess back through the first room of tables, past the arcade, and into the next large room, next to the bowling and the karaoke stage, a long table with Matt and his family sitting and having drinks.

"Here you are." The hostess sat us down and left.

Matt stood and greeted Roxy with a big hug. He said something to her, but I couldn't hear it. She smiled at him and replied,

"Thanks, Matt."

He shook Paul's hand and gave me a hug and a kiss on the cheek.

Paul's hand on mine grasped me a bit tighter!

Matt sat down, and Sara gave me a big hug. Paul had let my hand go, and I introduced him to Sara officially.

"This is Paul, my boyfriend."

"Nikki, he's cute!" She whispered to me.

Paul smiled, appreciating her enthusiasm for him.

"It's nice to finally meet you, Sara."

We met her friend Violet as well. Her brother Jagger wasn't here, and I didn't think Sara would have invited him, especially with her parents at the table.

Next up were Matt's parents, Griffin and Diane Stevens

Griffin Stevens was an older model of his son, his blond hair now darker with a mix of gray. Still athletic, once a quarterback for his college team back east, he held himself to a high degree of health.

His recent partnership with his law firm was the reason for the move to Las Vegas. His law firm is the leading firm that represents casinos and corporations in Nevada.

"Nikki, it's so nice to see you. It's been a year and a half, maybe?"

"I think you're right. Has it been that long? It's nice to see you."

He gave me a big hug.

"And this must be Paul?" They shook hands, "Let me introduce you to my better half here."

Matt's mom, Diane, came up to meet Paul, and she smiled.

"It's nice to meet you."

Yup, she was sizing him up, Diane Stevens, a beautiful platinum blond, a competitive, educated, athletic woman. Her love and joy are her family, and her work as one of the top architects in her field is her pride and motivation for her strength. Her blazing blue eyes, no doubt her son inherited them as well, became fierce and calculating when she spoke with Paul. I have to say Diane has always been very good to me; she has always given me respect and has been delightful, but at this moment, I knew she had become weary of Paul, almost territorial, because she knows her son is still in love with me. She turned to me and gave me a big hug. "Nikki, it's been too long. I want to thank you for everything you have done to help Sara. I'm glad you could join us this evening."

"I wouldn't have missed it."

We all sat back down. Now, the silence at the table was drowned out by the music from Tom Petty: "I Won't Back Down." Everyone hid behind the large menus; I glanced over at Paul, who seemed to be concentrating on the beer menu. Roxy nudged me in the ribs, a look of oh my gosh.

"Awkward!"

She mouthed in silence. I just nodded. I glanced over at Matt, and he looked over at me with a smile. I looked back down my menu and decided on the Cobb Salad.

Roxy and Violet ordered the BBQ burger with fries, and Paul and Matt ordered the French dip with a side salad. Sara went with the Mushroom and Swiss burger, and Matt's parents both ordered a steak with all of the trimmings.

Our server, a peppy young woman, brought out our drinks as well. The guys all ordered beers, and the gals went for lemonade, iced tea, and a champagne Bellini. Can you guys guess who ordered that? Yup, Matt's mom. I always make it a rule not to drink alcohol when I need to be extra sharp in the company of this party. Our appetizers arrived.

Next, a large plate filled with cheese, meats, pickles, olives, crackers, basically a nice charcuterie board, so to speak. We all placed food on our appetizer plates; the music churned out a new tune of "Eye of the Tiger" by Survivor.

My inner monologue began...

Ladies and gentlemen, in this corner, we have Diane the ball buster Stevens (cheers and clapping). In the next corner, we have Nikki Rodriguez, the challenger with the voice of a rock star. (Cheers and clapping) Round 1 - has started with the jarring expressions from Diane landing on Paul, the innocent bystander. Next, we see Nikki taking some action; she's coming up on the right, and it looks like she's going in for a jab.

This was the skit playing in my head right now. I had to take some control! I excused myself from the table for just a moment.

I found our server and politely asked her to put the bill on my credit card.

"I'll take care of the check for everyone."

I smiled.

"It's my treat."

"Wow, that's so cool, ok."

She took my card and added it to the bill to be charged as soon as we all finished. I took my card back and put it in my small wallet, and placed it back into my purse. I went back to the table, and Paul stood and pulled out my chair for me.

I noticed Diane watching our every move.

"Thank you, Paul. He's such a gentleman."

I said, taking my seat.

Sara was chatting about going back to school, and that Violet is going to see if Sara can try out for La Crosse. Violet was saying, One of the girls got hurt, and then one transferred out to another state, and they are down two girls; they don't have any reserve gals because of the new grading policy.

"You're a Stevens, of course, you'll be on the team. We have all been athletes in high school and college."

Griffin told us confidently.

"Paul, did you participate in athletics in school?"

Diane asked,

All eyes were on Paul now!

"I did. I was on varsity swim team in high school and four years swim team in college."

"You went to college, do most police officers do that?" Diane responded.

I was blindsided by her comment to Paul! *Round 2, Diane, the ball buster, takes another swipe at Paul, the innocent bystander.*

Paul responded to her, "Yes, ma'am, I have a degree in psychology. It helps in my line of work, many officers have degrees in criminology, sociology, business, communications, and many other fields."

"Well, that's good to know, and what college did you attend?"

"USC, go Trojans." Paul smiled.

"Oh, a rival! All of my sons attended UCLA, go Bruins."

Diane spread a sly smile upon her face.

"To be truthful, I left UCLA after my second year to transfer to Cal State Los Angeles because of their fire program; it's one of the best in the state!" Matt said.

Diane cut her steak, "If I recall, you were at the top of your class there."

The music changed to "TNT" by AC/DC. OK, ok, we were rocking into battle now!

"Nikki, thank God we went to a nice Catholic University." Roxy chimed in.

I nodded and smiled; I took another forkful of chicken and salad with a sweet tomato. I could at least enjoy my food.

"You two are good girls, the kind every mother wants to see her son with. We consider you part of the family, Nikki."

She looked over at Matt.

I smiled and nodded.

"You are right, my mother adores Nikki," Paul added to the conversation. He held my hand and gave it a light squeeze.

Round 3, ladies and gentlemen, goes to Paul, the innocent bystander.

"So, does that mean the two of you will be heading down the aisle soon?"

And the ball buster steps in for a surprise jab!

This caught Paul off guard; he realized the whole table had their attention on his response.

"I want to go play ski ball." Sara stood up, and she and Violet ran off

I was ready to run off, too; this was getting a little intense, and these weren't even my relatives.

Roxy looked sympathetic to Paul.

I was a deer in the headlights!

Matt looked worried, Griffin was curious, and the sly smile on Diane's face was epic. She cornered him and had him right where she wanted him.

On the spot!

Ever so cool and collected, Paul responded to Diane's question "Well, now, Diane, how did you know? I guess I might as well do it right here. I was planning a romantic weekend."

Paul smiled.

Diane gasped and looked over at Matt; he looked like he wanted to disappear. Roxy giggled, and I wanted to give Paul a big kiss! Griffin, the great guy I know, he is asked his wife to accompany him to play a round of ping pong. She obliged politely, and they excused themselves from our table.

Round 4, ladies and gentlemen, the winner by TKO, the innocent bystander by calling Diane's bluff, and we have a new champion tonight.

"You're the Best" by Joe Esposito from the Karate Kid movie began playing.

Matt waited until they left, and then he moved over to where Sara was sitting next to Roxy, "I just want to apologize to you all for my mother. Sometimes she can be very competitive. Honestly, I'm embarrassed!"

"Don't worry, Matt. We all have moms, don't sweat it, bro." Roxy nudged him in the arm.

"Matt, it's not your fault. Don't worry; I think your mom just felt a little threatened by me." Paul replied.

"I feel bad that she put both of you in an awkward position." Matt responded.

I was quiet during this time, and Roxy could see that I was replaying what happened in my head.

"Hey Paul, I bet I can beat you at that pinball game right over there."

"Oh, really, ok, you're on."

Roxy and Paul walked five feet from our table and started their game off at the Superman pinball machine.

"Just Waiting on a Friend" by The Rolling Stones began to play.

When they were out of earshot, Matt slid over one more chair.

"I'm sorry, Nikki, I feel terrible, maybe this is why I live far from my mom, she can be difficult."

"Well, it's like Roxy said, we have moms, and sometimes they overstep their boundaries."

The server arrived with the bill

Matt reached for it, "Nikki, it's on me."

"Too late, she already paid."

The server responded.

"I owe you, Nikki."

Matt replied with a feeling that I need to pay you back for the humiliation you had to endure.

"Don't worry about it. Still friends, right?"

I asked him.

"Yeah, still friends, always."

He replied with a smile.

Chapter 17

Valentine's Day

Last night, I had finally went to bed around 9:30, not too late, so I got at least eight hours of sleep. After Paul and I dropped off Roxy at her place, she sent me a text.

Thank you, girl, for inviting me to dinner. There was so much drama, I forgot about my breakup. And you know what's funny, I'm not that bothered by it Lol." Silly with the tongue-out emoji.

" Glad I could help my bestie." Lol, silly emoji with the Groucho Marks glasses.

Paul and I had a few moments kissing on the sofa, and then I insisted I needed to get some sleep; my day on Valentine's Day would be so busy.

"I'll come by at the end of the evening and pick you up."

He offered.

"Ok, we will be closing at midnight, but come by at 9 pm, and I can get away up to my office with you, and we can eat up there alone," I replied

"I'll be there."

He smiled. I locked the door behind him and then went off to change into my PJs.

My phone chimed again, the cupid's arrow sounded, and a new text message came.

It was from Sara,

"Oh my God, Nikki, I can't believe my mother, her behavior was so sus(used by this new generation for suspect) *earlier before dinner! And the moment I knew you were bringing Paul, I knew why. She and Matt had been having a conversation upstairs in his TV room, and of course, they didn't think I could hear them, but like I'm 15, I can spy better than anyone. Anywho, she was like being completely Matt, you need to settle down, and now you have this big house, you can have a family, what's going on? I thought you were serious with Nikki and stuff like that. She is a world-class nagger, and I knew she would do this to poor Matt. I mean, hello, he's only 30, it's not like he's old in his 50s or something. Dad doesn't say anything to Matt, but if he knew Mom was going to town on him, he would have told her to stop nagging Matt; he's a dude, and he will decide when he is ready to settle down. She was just lucky Dad was outside taking a call from his office. My poor bro, can you believe that? I'm glad they have an early flight at 7 am. Matt has to be at work at 6 am, so they are having a town car pick them up. Thank God Mom didn't meet Jagger, she would have been more of a mess!*

I replied to her:

"Don't worry, Sara; your mom is just a concerned mom; she wants her children to be happy. I'm fine and so is Paul, don't worry about it. Matt can take the heat, no pun intended. Lol, I know Matt is working tomorrow, so if you and your friends want to come to Kendle's for dinner, you can be my guest."

"Thanks, Nikki, we will do that. Jagger can drive us, and we can be there by 8:30. We're going to the arboretum for a concert from Dead Flys. They're a new rock band, and this is their first concert here. I'm so excited!

"Ok, see ya tomorrow, go to sleep," I replied.

"K C-ya," Sara said.

The sunny morning was chilly, and I had my coffee inside today and planned on taking my heavier coat to work.

When I arrived, the first shift was already prepping food for the lunch crowd; Chef Stark would be in later today for the second shift for dinner. We had prime rib, filet mignon, Porterhouse steaks, and King Salmon fresh from Alaska. I got a call coming in. I looked at the number, Freddie.

"Hello, Freddie?"

"Hi, Nikki, are we still good to go today?"

"Yes, we are."

Freddie and I had come up with a plan to get Bobby to give up his secret stash. The FBI agent friend of Paul's would be here at noon and park outback with a team recording our conversation with Bobby; they needed to get him to spill, and they would have more evidence besides the offshore accounts he had put in his girlfriend's name. They had most of what they needed, but were more apt to have a confession and to also see if there was more evidence of what he had done.

Right after I hung up with Freddie, I got a call from Marge down at the City Hall offices.

"What's up, Marge?"

"Nikki, I wanted to let you know, incoming at your restaurant, Stacie made reservations for this afternoon at 3:30 pm, she told me she was going with Paul to have a late lunch."

"Thanks, Marge, I'll handle it from here."

"Ok, bye-bye, dear."

Kendle's was looking like Cupid's palace. I had a local company bring in balloons in pink, red, and white; I had an arch of balloons at the front entrance and one in the ballroom, where we had more tables. I had balloons hanging from the ceiling and another balloon arch on the makeshift stage. Tonight, the plan was that we would be seating everyone in the ballroom aged 21 and over, and in the restaurant, we were going to sit families with children and guests 20 years old and under. The family area would have cool acts on stage from two local high schools, singers, dancers, and rock bands.

In the 21 and over banquet room, I had hired two bands, one 80s rock tribute band and Pink Stilettos, a band that played the Harvest festival back in October. Later on, the last act was Little Black Dress, featuring special guests Freddie Santana and Cold Creek.

Everything was in motion, and by 11 am, when we opened, we were slammed! I had all of my servers today on staff; it went by seniority. The lunch crew was the newbies, and tonight's servers were going to be the veteran servers who have been with Kendle's for years.

Tito and Daisy would be here this evening, so Ken took the love birds' shift during the day.

"For me, I prefer the day shift boss; I can take my girl out this evening to Malibu."

"Oh, Ken, Malibu does sound nice, and the surfing there is way cool!"

I thought of surfing, Paul and I are going to go up to Santa Barbara next week to surf and have a fun weekend. That sounded so good, a mini vacay.

I went to the hostess desk and logged into the white IPAD, sure enough, there in black and white was the reservation for Stacie Mc. Daniels, party of two, with special instructions for a table in the corner, a high back booth, and a chilled bottle of champagne, was requested along with a bowl of fresh chilled strawberries. She was planning a romantic lunch that was obvious and right under my nose.

At 2 pm, Freddie met me in my office, Diaz dressed like a busboy with another FBI agent, both undercover so Bobby wouldn't notice any heat!

"I'm wired, my cell phone is in my jacket pocket, how about you, Nikki?" Freddie asked.

"I'm ready. My cell phone is in my back pocket."

My black silk slacks held my phone and the app for spying. New technology, man, was it mind-blowing.

No wires anymore, and thank goodness for it, I don't know that my red chiffon blouse would have hidden a real wire.

Freddie walked back downstairs and met up with Bobby; I sat them at a table where they ordered drinks.

"Bobby, I have to tell you the reason why I left and what I came to realize."

Bobby was listening intently in his sharp grey Armani suit. Freddie was dressed in black jeans with a dark shirt and his black leather jacket. He spoke softly and then told Bobby they needed to go somewhere more private to talk. He told him that I owned the restaurant and they could continue their conversation upstairs. Bobby agreed, and I led them upstairs to my office!

"Bobby, Freddie, make yourselves at home; I have a full bar if you would like a drink."

"That won't be necessary, Nikki, thank you," Bobby replied.

I led them to my office and closed the door. I waited in the office's small lobby and pressed my ear to the door to hear their conversation.

When Bobby knew the coast was clear, he spoke.

"So what is this really about, Freddie?"

"It's about the fact that I know you are stealing from me and the band Bobby."

He chuckled. "What are you talking about?"

"You know what I'm talking about. I know you've been taking money and putting it in an offshore account in your girlfriend's name."

Bobby looked surprised. He took a deep breath before he spoke, collected himself, and then said,

"Who else knows about this?"

"No one, just me, I followed the trail you left."

"I didn't leave any trail. I was careful, and the money was paid to miscellaneous expenses. You probably found out from that ex-wife of yours she never trusted me anyway."

"You leave Jenny out of this, and you stay away from her."

Freddie was threatening. Pointing his finger at Bobby and puffing up his chest. The look of anger took hold of his face.

"Freddie, Freddie, let's be sensible, no one is going to hurt anyone!"

Bobby put some distance between himself and Freddie.

"Here's what's going to happen: I'm going to walk out of here, and you're going to forget about what I took, and after that, you'll never see me again!"

Freddie shook his head no, "Bobby, why did you do it? I thought we were good to you. Why did you steal from us?"

Bobby chuckled again, "Because it was so easy, you aging rockers, you think the music is all that matters! It's money, industry, you guys were big time back in the 70s, stick it to the man, but you made lots of money, what a bunch of hypocrites! You enjoyed the drugs, the girls, the fancy hotels, and the non-stop partying. Well, now it's my turn to enjoy that life, it's my money now! I'm not giving it back to a bunch of has-been geriatric rockers that still think they are relevant!"

"We may be guilty of all of that, but we worked for that money; for some of us, it comes with a cost; we paid with our families, relationships, and friendships, and some with their lives!"

"Well, I'm not going to have any loose ends. I'm taking my money, and I'm leaving with it."

I waited for Freddie to say the word that would send the FBI in, but I didn't hear it from him. Something was wrong! I rushed into the office to see Bobby holding onto Freddie with a gun to his chest.

"Bobby, what are you doing?"

He looked at me, and then Freddie belted him one in the jaw.

Bobby dropped the gun and went down. The FBI and Diaz came up the stairs and put their guns on Bobby.

"FBI, Bobby Williams, you are under arrest for embezzlement."

He was moaning and then picked up off the floor of my office, and then they began reading him his rights. He grunted, rubbing his jaw from the pain, cuffed and staggering, they walked him out. Paul's friend at the FBI walked over to us, "You did great. Freddie, we got everything. He's going away for a long time. We also recovered the money; it came to 5.7 million in a Swiss account." Freddie whistled in response to the amount of money that had been taken by Bobby.

Freddie turned to me, "Nikki, thank you for all of your help. I couldn't have done this without the help of your friends in law enforcement, too.

We walked downstairs to the kitchen; the Feds were taking Bobby into a waiting black van. Diaz took off his apron, put his white long-sleeved Oxford button-down shirt back on over his white t-shirt, and tucked it into his dark jeans. He left his sports coat hanging in the staff coat closet; there was no need for it in here. He went back to his post at the back of the kitchen.

The FBI drove away, and the small staff parking lot was free from anything that had just taken place.

Chef Stark walked into the kitchen's back door. "Was that an FBI van out there?"

"I'll see you later tonight, Nikki."

Freddie left out the back door.

I waved bye and then led Chef Stark to his office,

"Tony, let me tell you what happened."

Chapter 18

Be Mine

The lunch crowd had me running back and forth, playing the role of hostess along with being the general manager today.

Everyone loved the decor, and the balloon arches were a big hit! It was nearly 3:30 pm; the champagne bucket sat next to the table with a bottle of Taittinger Cuvee Prestige Rose, $100.00 per bottle; she was going all out.

I set the champagne flutes at the place setting and the chilled crystal bowl of fresh organic strawberries in the center of the table.

I stood at the front desk and gave my hostess her lunch break. I wanted to be the face Stacie saw and the one to be front and center when she tried her stunt.

I knew Paul was a great guy; his love for me was true, and he would let Stacie down gently.

They walked in together. Stacie plastered a great big smile on her face, and she walked confidently up to the front hostess desk, her light pink tight dress clinging to her curves, her long dark hair cascading down her back.

The hot pink stilettos sparkled from the studded rhinestone jewels on them. They were very cute; I saw a pair of them at Macy's last week. I believe they're made by INC.

Of course, she also had a plunging neckline showcasing her diamond-crusted heart necklace and her boob job.

Paul was looking extremely uncomfortable, dressed in his grey suit with a white starched dress shirt and no tie.

His black Oakley sunglasses on his beautiful greenish blue eyes, and his dark hair sleek and in place. Boy, is he dreamy!

"Happy Valentine's Day."

I said as they walked up to the desk. Paul smiled at me, and I smiled back, never letting my eyes drift from his. He took off his sunglasses, and I was lost in his presence.

I pulled two menus from the small shelf under the desk and led them to their table.

He had called me 1/2 hour before they arrived to tell me that Stacie had invited him to lunch here and that he was well aware of her desire to get back together with him.

He told me he would gently make her understand that he was only interested in me and that this crush of hers had to come to an end. He is always so honest, and I thanked my lucky stars I was with him.

"Here you are, your server will be here in just a moment," I said as they sat in the high-back booth. I popped the champagne cork with a cloth napkin over it to prevent spillage and a flying cork! I had become such a pro at this. Although in my alternate universe, the cork popped Stacie right in the chest, and lo and behold, it bounced off and landed in another customer's cheesecake.

My little evil fantasy set me in a better mood, but instead, I simply poured the champagne and then placed it back in the bucket. And walked back to the kitchen. But not before Stacie made her toast.

"Here is to friendship, love, and world peace."

Oh my God, seriously! I rolled my eyes when I was out of sight. My hostess finished her break and went back to her station, and I went to seat more customers.

One customer next to their booth spilled a glass of wine; I began to clean it up by bringing a few towels to soak up the spill on the wood floor, thank goodness it's a high-quality laminate.

Stacie saw me cleaning the mess, so she spoke so I could hear her every word. I wanted to leave, but the customer who spilled their drink insisted I give them a rundown of the desserts and how they are made.

I wanted to be out of earshot, but fate had other plans for me. This is how it went...

Stacie began. "Paul, I asked you to lunch because I felt compelled to be honest with you. I have to get this out, and this might be the only way that I can." She put on the charm, her doe eyes innocent and pleading.

Paul sat still, listening, analyzing the situation; he remained cool.

Stacie took a long drink of champagne, nearly finishing the pink bubbly off.

She poured another glass for herself and continued.

"Paul, you know that we have an amazing friendship, and I have to admit I took this job to be closer to you. I can't deny it!"

She held up her hand.

"When we broke up, I had some time to reflect on it, and I realized it was the wrong move. I was wrong to break up with you because of your demanding job.

You needed someone understanding, and I wasn't. I know how much you love being a cop.

It's who you are, I know that now! I still love you, and I think that we should give ourselves that chance to start over and be the fabulous couple that we are."

Paul had been listening patiently while she carried on and saw me in his peripheral vision, and now it was his turn to respond.

"Stacie, we have been friends for a long time, and when we broke up, I had time to reflect, too.

I dated other women, and I moved away from LA. For me, it was the best move I made. I am happy here in Rancho Niguel. I have friends and a great job, and I found someone special.

My relationship with Nikki is still new, but we have a wonderful connection, and I have fallen in love with her. I can't hurt her; I know we were both in love, too! But since you left, my heart belongs to Nikki.

I can always be your friend and be there if you need any help, but I need to keep our relationship strictly as friendship."

This was not the news Stacie thought she was going to hear; she had a single tear running down her cheek. My guess now was that she would leave Paul alone and move on.

Stacie smiled through it and replied,

"I understand, Paul."

Paul got up from the booth.

"I need to get back to work; I can drop you off at your office."

"That's ok, I'm going to finish my drink and call an Uber."

Paul took the champagne bottle from the bucket, handed it to a server who was passing by, and asked her to dispose of it.

"I'm not going to let you get drunk and feel twice as bad tomorrow. Come on."

He smiled that sincere, sweet smile that always warms my heart.

I finished going over the dessert menu for the couple at their table and passed by their booth, heading for the hostess desk.

Paul helped Stacie up; she was already tossed, and he looked concerned.

They were near the front door when Stacie saw me at the hostess's desk, and she turned to Paul and planted a kiss on him. Paul pulled away fast!

"Stacie, please stop this."

Paul's phone rang; it was the job.

"I have to take this." He stepped a few feet away.

Stacie turned, walked to the hostess desk, pointed to me, and whispered, "This isn't over, Nikki. You took something from me, and I'm going to get it back."

I didn't say anything to her; I didn't want a scene in front of my customers.

Paul was finished with his call and came back. "Let's go, Stacie." He led her out of the restaurant and looked back at me. He mouthed, "Call you later."

I simply waved.

Chapter 19

Sweethearts

Roxy walked in around 5:15 pm, and I was dying to tell her what happened this afternoon. I gave her the scoop about the FBI and Bobby getting arrested and how Freddie belted him one in the jaw when Bobby had pulled a gun on him.

We enjoyed a quick glass of wine as we sat in the back of the kitchen by Diaz; he had a Coke.

"Oh my gosh, Nikki, that's wild. So what happened to Freddie? Did he get his money back?"

Diaz answered her question.

"Right now, it's in a safe place and will be returned soon. Of course, there will be a big case that will take care of the criminal side of it, and Freddie and his band can sue for the damages.

"Wow, that's mind-blowing!" Roxy said.

Diaz had to take a call from the PD, so he went to Chef Stark's office. Now that Roxy and I were alone, I filled her in on the Stacie and Paul drama.

I told her how I had to listen to their conversation because Stacie was louder than usual, and I had to clean up after the couple that spilled the wine, and then they insisted I give them every bit of information on the dessert menu.

"Girl, you crack me up. Any other woman would have wanted a front-row seat to this daytime drama."

"Honestly, I feel bad for being there!"

"True, I mean, after he let her down easy, she was probably ready to tear your hair out.

"That is true!" I agreed.

Then I told her what Stacie did next, how Paul responded so cool and calmly, and how he was such a gentleman to her when she laid that big kiss on him that he backed away from.

"Boy, that woman is trouble! I can't believe she blames you for Paul falling in love with you. You met him way after she broke up with him, and you didn't even know her."

Roxy said, giving her opinion.

"I think she's very unstable; she was totally trashed from the champagne. Can you imagine what poor Paul has had to deal with? She's an alcoholic, and this is the second episode since she's been here where Paul had to help her out of a restaurant!"

I told Roxy.

We both shook our heads at the thought of what she had done.

"I really think you should tell Paul what she said. That kind of threat is serious, and now she's hurting from the big disappointment from lunch today."

"Yeah, you have a good point there! I will tell Paul because now he will see that she can be dangerous.

I bet she's the one behind all of the sabotage to the Youth Center and the damage to my car, the attempt on my life with a nail gun! I know she's the one doing it, I just have to catch her in the act!"

"You just need to watch your back, too, lady. Because if she threatened you two feet away from Paul, she is capable of more!"

I looked at my watch: 5:45 pm, we'd better get moving, the Valentine's Dinner will begin soon.

Roxy and I checked and double-checked the main dining room and the banquet room; everything was ready. At 6 pm sharp, our doors opened to families waiting to enter. Each family with kids received a box of candy conversation hearts from Sweethearts.

The banquet room holding the 21-and-over party was set to begin at 9 pm; the decor was spot on. Each place setting on the tables in the banquet room had a tiny red box with a single chocolate raspberry truffle in it.

Roxy and I manned the front desk and seated our guests.
Wonderful plates of steaks, chicken, and pasta were served, and
our desserts decorated the room on a large table buffet style.
By 8:30 pm, Sara and Jagger came in, holding hands, acting
playful and giddy. Sara was beaming.

She was dressed in a short but tasteful black dress; she wore her
dark hair up with curls. Her beautiful blue eyes sparkled with joy.
Jagger was a handsome dude, at six feet tall, he wore his black
sports coat like a model in an ad for cologne. His jet-black hair
gelled back; he resembled a young Elvis. The gorgeous couple in
all black looked glamorous! Sara also wore a pink rose corsage on
her wrist! "Isn't it beautiful? He's so thoughtful." Sara kissed him
on the cheek. They were so cute!

"Let me show you to your table." I took them to a nice table with a
window view of the mountains, quiet and away from the young
kiddies. "The two of you are my special guests. Order whatever
you like; it's on the house."

"Wow, thank you, Ms. Nikki, you *are* the coolest!" Jagger said,
smiling and thanking me.

"Thanks, Nikki," Sara said, beaming.

As I walked away, Sara said, "Didn't I tell you she's the coolest?"
I left the love birds to their dinner, and I went to go check on the
kitchen.

Diaz had left three hours ago; I told Paul, with so many people here, no one was going to try to do me in with so many witnesses. Besides, he would be here in half an hour, and he was staying with me until closing.

The family dining was winding down, and now just 10 tables were filled with families finishing up. I took this time to run upstairs to my office and put my feet up for a 15-minute break.

I reached the top of the stairs to a breathtaking sight.

The lobby furniture was moved aside, and before me sat a lovely dinner for two of Porterhouse steaks, baked potatoes with all the fillings, and an arugula salad with feta and dried cranberries, all placed on the coffee table. Two large pillows sat on the lobby rug that I had under the coffee table. Three tall vases of red roses were placed where the sofa was. The lights were dimmed low, and greeting me with a big smile was Paul.

"This is absolutely beautiful!"

"Happy Valentine's Day." He kissed me.

He opened a bottle of Australian Shiraz, poured two glasses, and we toasted. "Here's to us," I said.

"To us." He replied.

"When did you have time to put all of this together?"

"I got off work a little early; I also had your excellent chef's help with this, too."

"Oh, well, this is just beautiful, thank you."

"I thought you could use a nice break."

We ate our dinner and chatted about the lovely roses that filled my office with their sweet scent. We didn't talk about work, Stacie, or any other issues going on in Rancho Niguel.

We discussed our Hawaii trip coming up in June. Back in December, I had won a raffle for a trip to the Big Island, and I upgraded our package with five-star accommodations and first-class flights. I had given the trip to Paul as a Christmas gift with the promise of getting me into a swimsuit for a seven-day vacation in paradise.

"I can see the waves already and the sandy beaches," Paul said, envisioning our trip.

"And don't forget the Pina Coladas for me."

I added.

We lay on our sides on the pillows, facing each other, lost in our discussion of Hawaii. I snuggled closer to him and put my head on his chest, his heartbeat steady and strong. He wrapped his arms around me, lifted my chin, and we kissed.

Chapter 20

Duets

After our dinner, Paul and I cleaned up the lobby and went
downstairs. The 21-and-over party was already jumping.

I checked on the family dining, and the staff was closing up that
half of the restaurant.

Sara had sent me a text thanking me for the spectacular dinner.

*Nikki, it was so good, we had the Wild King Salmon with the rice
pilaf. Boy, does Chef Stark know how to cook! Jagger was so
impressed! Thank you again, Nikki, I owe ya, babe!*

I responded.

I'm glad you two had a great time!

Roxy came by and let me know we would go on stage in fifteen
minutes. " Nikki, we're on in 15, girl."

I changed into my little black dress, black stilettos, and red lipstick
quickly, with Paul zipping me up as we entered the banquet room.
The tables of pink linens and white tablecloths were cute, red
flowers in heart-shaped vases as centerpieces, and a grand buffet
table lined the side of the room. The dance floor filled with people

dancing to Pink Stilettos singing, "I'll be there for you." By Bon Jovi.

Martin and Oliver walked up to Paul and me, "Hi guys, I feel like I haven't seen you in forever." Oliver air-kissed my cheek

"You look beautiful as always, Nikki." Martin complimented.

"Paul, good to see you."

Oliver said.

"Good to see you both."

Paul replied.

"Well, guys, I have to go to work."

I excused myself and went up on stage.

"She's been working all day."

Paul chimed.

I was handed the mic from the lead singer of Pink Stilettos, and I opened the event.

"Let's have another big round of applause for Pink Stilettos."

Everyone cheered and clapped.

"I'd just like to say to everyone, Happy Valentine's Day."

I got a big cheer from the crowd.

I saw Craig and Kiana, Mrs. Green, Marge, and Betty Jean with their boyfriends, Sonya and her husband Charlie, and, of course, many other people from the community.

We had a full house!

"Ladies and gentlemen, before we perform, I'd like to introduce some special guests that we are going to jam with."

Everyone looked puzzled; I could see people saying who is the special guest, what a surprise, who is it? Who's here?

"I'd like to introduce my friends Freddie Santana and Cold Creek."

There were cheers and clapping, a lot of wows, and no way, cool! Freddie and his band came up on stage and mixed in with Little Black Dress. I took my place up front at the mic, and Freddie joined me. We started with one of their first and most popular songs, Little Bit O' Love, from the early 1970s.

We rocked three more songs, two of Cold Creek's and one slow song duet by Stevie Nicks and Don Henley, "Leather and Lace."

Freddie and I sat on high stools, looking out at the audience. We sang our duet and received cheering, clapping, and even whistles. After the last guest went home, Freddie, Cold Creek, and Little Black Dress packed it up.

"Nikki, me and the band just want to thank you for the help you and your friends gave us."

Freddie said sincerely.

"Next time we're in town, I'm gonna want some of that Chile Chocolate cake," T-bone said.

"It's funny you said that. I ran to the kitchen and removed a to-go box from the fridge.

"T-bone, here is some cake to go."

"Wow, Nikki, thanks," T-Bone said, hugging me.

Boss, Parker, and Flick gave me hugs and high-fived Paul.

We waved them off as they drove away in their travel bus on their way to Arizona.

Paul and I walked to his car, and we drove back to my place. The night was a bit chilly, so we turned on the fireplace. We enjoyed a glass of bourbon in front of the roaring fire. And some much need alone time.

Chapter 21

Hot Stuff

The next morning, I slept in. Valentine's Day had passed, and I was glad for that. Cupid had been very nice to me this year, and I was ready to move on. I had passed out all of the Sees candy bars and chocolates from Craig's nieces' fundraiser to my staff before they went home last night. Attached to them were pink envelopes filled with $300.00 cash as a bonus for their help last night.

My thoughts ran through the last couple of weeks' events: The incidents at the Youth Center, the floors being ruined, the nail gunning, the punch fountain breaking, and my car being demolished!

Were we any closer to finding the culprit?

I decided to fill my tub with rose bath oil and take some time to soak and relax. I lit my iced teaberry candles from American Lite, which I purchased from Kiana last summer. I put some tunes on Soft rock ballads.

The sweet scent from my bath drifted to me, and the light steam from the warm water calmed my muscles. Today, Kendle's wasn't open. Usually, I open only for dinner on Mondays, but when we have a big party, I give my staff some time to rest, and Chef usually has Monday and Tuesday off. My mind turned over some of the clues again,

The punch fountain breaking

The floors being vandalized

The nail gun incident

The lie about Flame

My car destroyed

But then I started to think about the mysteries from the last 6 months.

The press found out about the Vampire bites on Cat when she was murdered back in October.

The press got the jump on the Russian gun dealer back in December.

The pipes bursting at Kendle's before the Christmas Party!

Who was behind all of the sabotage?

All of these problems started when Stacie Mc. Daniels arrived! I couldn't call Paul; I knew he didn't think she was the one behind all of these incidents. No, I had to do my own investigation! After my bath, I got dressed, I put on a pair of skinny jeans and some tan Uggs, threw on a cream-colored sweater, and dried and styled my hair. I put on some quick makeup, and then, as I was getting ready to leave, my cell rang out.

I didn't bother looking at the number; I assumed it was Paul.

"Hi!" I enthusiastically blurted out.

"Uh, is this Ms. Rodriguez?"

"Yes, this is she."

"Ms. Rodriguez, this is Inspector 1543 Davidson with the City of Rancho Niguel. I'm here at Kendle's restaurant for an inspection. Can someone let me in?"

"I'm sorry, but usually we are closed on Mondays, but I can be down there in 10 minutes. I do apologize."

"No problem, I'll be waiting at the back door by the kitchen."

"Ok, I'm on my way." I hung up, put my phone in my pocket, and grabbed my keys to the rental jeep along with my wallet. I was out the door in a flash!

I thought about waiting for Diaz; he was going to be here in about 10-15 min, so I sent him a text telling him where I would be.

Hi Diaz,

I had a health inspector call me; I have to be at Kendle's right now to open for the inspection. Meet me there.

Thanks

Nikki

He replied

Negative Nikki,

Paul would want you to wait for me.

Jay, I'm already here!

I arrived at Kendle's; I parked in the back in my usual parking stall. I got out of the jeep, tucked my phone in my back pocket, and searched for the inspector. I didn't see anyone around, and the parking lot was empty. I thought maybe he parked out front on the street and walked over here; maybe he was sitting in his car! It seemed strange!

I began walking towards the back door, and I was almost there when Oliver called out to me from across the street.

"Nikki, I need to talk to you."

He waved to me.

I turned quickly and jogged over toward Oliver when, all of a sudden, an explosion went off! The ground shook, and the next thing I knew, I fell to the ground and rolled by my rental car. I opened my eyes to see Oliver come over and kneel down next to me.

"Nikki, Nikki." His words were far away and muffled. I saw him on his cell and heard him say, "Help, my friend was just near an explosion at Kendle's restaurant, hurry, send a fire truck, send an ambulance, please hurry."

Oliver was in tears now.

"My friend Nikki Rodriguez she's hurt!"

In the distance, I heard fire truck sirens and police sirens coming toward Oliver and me. He had put his jacket under my head and was holding my hand. He then told me, "Nikki, help is coming." I heard the fire truck stop, and I could hear Matt telling his crew what to do. He rushed over to me with Anita and James right behind him. My eyes closed.

"Nikki, baby, wake up." I heard Matt tell me.

Chapter 22

Stupid Cupid

My sweater had been cut open, and I was on a gurney in an ambulance. My chest was thrust up, and a defibrillator brought me back! Paul and Matt were both in the ambulance with me. The doors closed, and we raced to the hospital.

Later on, I woke up in a hospital room, clothed in a hospital gown, feeling extremely sore everywhere. My hand had an IV in it, rendering me fluids, and a nurse was adjusting my pillow for me.

"What happened? Where am I?" I spoke, my throat feeling scratchy and sore.

"Try to rest, Ms. Rodriguez; you've had quite a morning. Do you remember what happened?" She asked.

"I remember the explosion at my restaurant, and then the ambulance took me away."

I shook my head, indicating that was all.

"Your heart stopped twice, once on the way here and then as soon as you arrived.

Looks like you'll make a full recovery, though, with no future damage, and you didn't need surgery; you were very lucky.

The doctor will be in soon; she's checking on a patient. You have a full house of friends out there waiting to see you."

"I do."

"Yeah, you came with a fireman and a police detective; they were so worried about you."

The door opened, and the doctor came in.

"Hi, I'm Doctor Hudson."

She looked like she was 25 years old, if that, wearing light green scrubs with a stethoscope around her neck.

"We had to bring you back twice from cardiac arrest due to the blast. The good news is you're going to make a full recovery, and there is no permanent damage to your heart. It's very strong. It's a good thing you're in great shape and healthy. We did run a few tests, and we will run some more in the next few days, and then you can go home. I'll have you come back in one week just as a follow-up, but other than that, what you need is rest. So I'll send up some food for you, and I think your friends are anxious to see you."

"Thank you."

I replied.

She walked out with the nurse; I heard her say only two at a time and make it brief: she needs to rest.

Paul and Roxy came into the room.

"Oh, Nikki, I'm so glad you're ok." Roxy hugged me.

"Thanks, Roxy."

"I'm going to go and let you and Paul have some time to talk."

As soon as Roxy left, Paul kissed me.

"Thank God you're alright. I was so scared."

"You can't get rid of me that easily." I smiled.

"Do you remember what happened?"

I searched my memory for an answer: "I remember getting a phone call from an inspector from the city to inspect the restaurant."

"Diaz gave me your message; I wish you had waited for him!" Paul scolded me.

"I know!"

I continued with my story.

"I drove over to Kendle's, but I didn't see anyone there.

I was going to the back door when Oliver saw me and called me over.

So I jogged towards him and then boom, this bright light went off and then a big bang, and it felt like an earthquake right under my feet, then I fell, and then the sirens and the ambulance, and that's all, it's still a blur."

"Don't worry, I'll find the person who did this."

Paul's eyes looked tired, but were filled with ice when he promised to find the culprit.

He kissed me again, his eyes warm.

I had a knock on the door; Matt came in.

"I'm so glad you're ok."

Matt ran to me, and then he held my hand to his face.

The ice in Paul's eyes came back!

***

As promised by my doctor, I was released from the hospital three days later. Roxy picked me up from the hospital; I had her bring me some clothes because mine were destroyed in my accident.

I put on a pair of jeans and a black tank top with a black and white striped button-down shirt. She even brought me some shoes since my Uggs were ruined with soot on them from the blast.

I had flowers in vases, flowers with stuffed animals, flowers from the Mayor, and even Freddie Santana and Cold Creek sent me a large arrangement with a big card that sent their love.

We packed it all in Beulah, the minivan we use for our equipment. Luckily, everything fit.

I thanked my nurses and doctors and waved to them, and then Roxy wheeled me out of the hospital doors. Hospital rules: you have to go out the door in a wheelchair, right?

Once we were in her car with our seatbelts fastened, she softly said, "Okay, spill it, what happened between you and Paul?"

Chapter 23

Be My Ex

I took a deep breath and began my story.

"Paul came by yesterday afternoon; I was feeling pretty good, you know, well rested and ready to go home the next day. He told me Kendle's is a total loss; the fire inspectors found that the culprit was C-4, which was placed outside the back of the restaurant, right by the back door.

Half the kitchen burned down, and the water damage from putting out the fire was just too much. So he asked me the usual, you know, did you notice anything suspicious?

He said he traced the call to a burner phone; they found it in a trash can about a mile down the road! He told me there was no inspector from the city, and someone set me up, and if it wasn't for Oliver, I wouldn't be here.

So then I told him I felt that Stacie was responsible for all of this! He said it was impossible! He said he was having coffee with her when he got the call that the restaurant had blown up!

He defended her the whole time. He said she called him and apologized for her actions on Valentine's Day; she spilled her guts, she said she was being foolish and disrespectful to me, and she swore she would stop drinking.

He swears she is completely innocent! So I got mad and told him to trust me, she is behind this, maybe she had someone help her with this, and the coffee meeting was to give her an alibi.

Then he got upset and told me I don't let him do his job and that I don't trust him. He told me I was *obsessing* over Stacie and that I was worried over nothing. Then, if that wasn't bad enough, he brought Matt into this.

He said if he were a jealous guy, he would have put a stop to Matt coming around a long time ago. Then he said Nikki, make a decision, me or him."

"He gave you an ultimatum?"

Roxy was surprised.

"I told him don't make me end my friendship with anyone in my life, and he got upset and said that maybe he wasn't as important in my life as he thought. He said maybe it was best that we go our separate ways, and before I could say anything else, he walked out my door."

"Whoa." That was all Roxy could say.

"Stupid Cupid made a fool of me."

"Yeah, both of us!"

Roxy said, speaking of her breakup as well.

I was so lost in my story, I didn't even realize we had been sitting in the car for the last ten minutes outside my condo.

I opened the door, and we walked to my place.

I unlocked the front door, and everyone yelled,

"Surprise!"

I was a little taken aback, surprised that was for sure!

My condo was filled with my friends laughing and cheering for my homecoming. A welcome home sign hung above the fireplace, yellow balloons floated from the ceiling, and yellow and pink streamers draped across the room. Almost everyone was here, Martin and Oliver, Mrs. Green, Marge and Betty Jean, Craig and Kiana, Daisy and Tito, Ken, Chef Stark, Jessica, and my band gals, Taylor, Dana, Emily, Matt, and Sara.

"Thank you, everyone, this is lovely."

I made my rounds, hugging my friends and thanking them for coming.

The table had food and desserts, all of my favorites: pies, chocolate cake, and cheesecake.

I sat at the head of the table, enjoying everyone's company, and the conversation switched to what was going to happen to Kendle's

"Are you going to rebuild?"

Jessica asked.

"Do you think they will find out who did this?"

Martin inquired.

Everyone had an opinion, and they picked Craig's brain to find their answers. No one mentioned Paul. Jessica had been lucky to visit yesterday, right after my breakup, and she knew the whole story, too.

I assumed she gently mentioned to everyone that Paul and I had broken up and that it would be best not to mention him because no one did.

I had told everyone about going out of town for a week,

"I'm going to see my mom and stepdad in a few days, and we are going to decide what to do with Kendles."

Matt turned to me, looking confused.

"Wait a minute, you own Kendle's?"

He was surprised.

"Yes, I'm a part owner with my stepdad; we have a business partnership."

Everyone nodded.

"Oh yeah, that's old news!"

Roxy said, adding a large piece of chocolate cake to her plate.

"Well, I didn't know."

Matt seemed a little bothered, but let it go.

"Don't forget the real estate agency, too; you're my boss."

Betty Jean piped up. Everyone agreed, but Matt seemed left out.

He quickly changed the subject and asked about

My car.

"So, have you decided what kind of car to purchase?"

"I'm not sure yet; I'm going to go shopping for one."

"Can I go with you?"

Sara asked with excitement.

"Sure!"

I smiled.

"You know my sweet 16th birthday is coming up, and I've already asked Mom and Dad for a car."

"Sara, maybe you should get your license first."

Matt reminded her.

"I will; I'm taking driver's training next semester."

She answered, and then she continued.

"Yeah, I thought the jeep we rented was cool, it was better than the minivan they had available, and remember that guy at the car rental company, wow, you guys, he was so funny."

Everyone listened with enthusiasm to Sara's story; she had everyone laughing.

Matt looked like he was missing something; he was listening to Sara's story, but he didn't say anything.

He looked over at me with concern on his face.

Oh man, I knew what he was thinking. Sara had spilled the story without realizing it; she wasn't supposed to have been with me at that time before she told her parents she would surrender to Matt's place when she had run away.

I was caught, and now he knew the truth. He was quiet for the remainder of the night. He didn't say any more to me; he just had casual conversations with everyone else, but I knew, I knew I had messed up.

Matt and Sara were the last to leave, but before they left, he asked to speak to me. He had Sara wait in the truck and said he would just be a few minutes.

Sara smiled and teased us, "Ok, you two keep it PG."

She went out to Matt's red truck and sat in the passenger seat.

He closed the door, and then he began telling me how he felt.

"Nikki, please tell me you didn't lie to me when you told me two weeks ago that you would let me know if my sister came to you?"

He asked me with conviction.

"Oh, no, don't do this to me!"

I began to walk away, but he followed and stood in front of me

"Please, Nikki, tell me the truth."

His blue eyes were calm, but the tension was building in him.

I had to come clean; I was caught, and I had to face the music. I put my hands up in defeat and then told him, not looking at him but turning my back to him.

"She came to me a few days after I left your house; she made me promise not to tell you she was with me. I just wanted to help her stay safe, and I thought if she was with me, she was ok."

I turned around to face him.

"I'm sorry, but I couldn't tell you."

"You lied to me."

He was upset now, and our eyes locked onto each other.

"I kept a promise to Sara,"

I told him sincerely.

"What about the promise you made to me?"

He pointed to himself; I was silent.

He shook his head and then said,

"I've been so stupid!"

He raked his hands through his hair in frustration.

"Look, you are important to me!"

I reached out to touch his shoulder, but he pulled away.

"Our friendship is very..."

I trailed off because he interrupted with

"Nikki, just save it, I feel like such an idiot chasing after someone who doesn't care about me."

He paced back and forth slowly, choosing his words carefully.

"Matt, that's not true, please don't say that, I broke up with Paul because he asked me to stay away from you."

I said, raising my voice, my eyes teared up, and I felt so sad.

He looked at me with pity,

"It's too late, Nikki, it's too late."

He turned and walked out the door.

After Matt left, I closed the door and went to the couch, and I felt like my heart would stop again.

Chapter 24

Kendle's

Only I, Nikki Rodriguez, could lose two guys in two days!

The next couple of weeks, I was busy making decisions with my family about Kendle's, Jeff and I decided to rebuild Kendle's and make it even better.

We met with an architect and went over my ideas for a two-story restaurant with an even larger banquet room to accommodate up to 500 people.

The land that Kendle's sat on was large enough to include a garden area for small luncheons, parties, and outdoor ceremonies.

We agreed on water elements, a man-made and very small-scale waterfall that would drop into a small pool that flowed from the garden to the downstairs patio dining.

The plans that the architect came up with were brilliant. We also had a decorator meet with us and show us the color scheme for the interior of the new place.

I wanted to add a surf or beach vibe to the place as an ode to California, with a touch of vintage Route 66.

We went with natural wood, light blues, white, and cream, with greenery from large plants, palm trees, and planters with birds of paradise in bright orange and fuchsia pink. The outside would have shiplap siding with navy trim and lots of glass windows. On the patio would be a fire pit for guests to sit by. Fountains in the courtyard and a large bar.

The restaurant would have a wall of windows and sliding doors that we could open. Terrace seating upstairs, so we would have the best views of the sunsets and the mountains.

The insurance took care of the damages, so financing for the rebuild was secured. I traveled with Mom and Jeff to Lake Tahoe for a late winter getaway.

I spent some time skiing on the slopes with them and relaxed in the hot tub. We had some laughs, and we had some of Jeff and Mom's friends over for a party of 30 at the chateau, but I wasn't in much of a party mood.

After my time in Tahoe, I came back to Rancho Niguel. My condo was stuffy, so I opened all of the windows and did some early Spring cleaning.

I checked out more cars online and took a few test drives, but I still hadn't decided on what to get.

A day later, early afternoon, I walked over to the burned-out building that used to be Kendle's.

The lot was set to be cleared tomorrow, so I sat on the short brick wall that bordered the old back patio. I sat there thinking about the crime, just going over it in my head. C-4 was placed on the back door.

How would Stacie have access to C-4, and how would she know how to use it? I kept putting everything together, but nothing seemed to fit. I kept going in circles and coming back with nothing. I walked around the debris, I kicked a few pieces of burned-out wood, and then something caught my eye.

I saw just a bit of it; a piece of drywall was partially covering it. I picked up the scorched drywall and tossed it away, and underneath it was my marble cupid.

It was fully intact and just dirty from soot. I picked it up and took it home with me.

The next day, I decided I needed a vehicle, and now!

Roxy had returned the Jeep when I was in the hospital, and miraculously, there was no damage to it.

I decided to narrow it down to my top three: the Mustang convertible, the Jeep Wrangler Rubicon, and my mother's pick, a convertible BMW; the last one wasn't going to happen!

I can't justify that cost; even the cheap series wasn't so cheap, and even though it wasn't about the money, it just didn't suit me.

So, between the Mustang and the Jeep, I had some shopping to do.

The next day, I walked across to the mall to see Martin and Oliver.

They asked me to come by and wear sandals. Hmm, what is that

about? When I came out of my place, I ran into Craig.

"Hi Craig, hey, is there any more information about the explosion

at Kendle's?"

Craig had his gym bag in his hand.

 "I'm on my way to work out; I can have the detective on the case

call you, Nikki. It's not my case, so I don't really know very much.

"Ok, thanks,"

I told him.

He hesitated as if he wanted to say something, he walked away and

then came back.

"I think it's a real shame what happened to your restaurant; it was a

nice place."

He said with real feeling.

"Thank you, Craig. Have a good workout."

 He looked at me sympathetically and went on his way in his royal

blue Dodge Challenger.

Chapter 25

Cheer up

I walked into the Dunner Art Gallery, and Martin was with a customer, looking at a beautiful painting.

Oliver walked up to me and gave me a big hug.

"Ok, Nikki, Martin is almost finished with our last customer, and then we are going to have a night out with you! You need some cheering up, and Martin and I are taking you for some mani-pedis, and then we are going to Blue 7 for drinks! Now, don't say no, we have been planning this for the last two days."

"Ok," I agreed. Defeated!

"We're going to turn that frown into a smile, I promise." Oliver said.

After the last customer left, they locked up, and we went out the back door to the gallery parking lot.

"When did you guys get the new car?"

I asked as I opened the door and slid into the pearl-white back seats as soft as butter.

We drove off in their brand new Range Rover Autobiography in Lantau Bronze. What a beauty!

"Last week, we needed a new car. The Audi was already ten years old, and we needed more room for picking up supplies. This one has a lot of room, so it seemed like the right move."

"Very classy, I approve, fellas."

I stated, still rubbing the soft leather backseat.

"We just love it, Nikki. You should take a look at them."

"It's beautiful, but I don't think I would put my surfboard back here with sand on it."

We went into Happy Day Spa for our mani-pedis. I got comfortable in the large massage chairs while my toes were painted in a red rose. The wax paraffin felt soothing on my achy feet, and my hands looked new and rejuvenated.

After I dried my nails, I put my high-heeled sandals back on. I did feel better already; never underestimate the effect of a mani-pedi! When we were finished, we drove over to Blue 7, the hottest bar in town right now. We got a table right away since it was a Wednesday night and not a big crowd.

We started with drinks: a Bloody Mary for me and two white wines for Martin and Oliver. We ordered some dinner and had time before it arrived to chat.

"So, Nikki, how are you doing?"

Martin asked me.

"Well, I'm single again!

I think I'll stay that way for a while and focus on re-opening Kendle's, and honestly, guys, I don't want to date for a long time. I think right now I'm going to be ok, just being with me."

I took a drink. Martin and Oliver frowned.

"Don't worry, Nikki; Matt has been a close friend for a while, he won't be upset for long,"

Martin said.

"It's ok, guys; I don't blame him for being upset, I can see his point, he thinks I betrayed him by keeping Sara's whereabouts from him. That's understandable, but for Paul to take Stacie's side. That hit me hard!

I still can't believe he took her side over mine. I guess I should have just been honest with myself first and foremost. He *was* my rebound. Matt and I had broken up, and it had only been a month, and then I stumbled onto Paul.

It was too fast, and I knew it."

"I am disappointed in Paul."

Martin said, taking a drink.

"Me too!" I agreed.

"That bitch Stacie!"

Oliver replied, taking a drink.

"She certainly has Paul in a tight grip!"

I said.

"We are supposed to be cheering you up; this is turning into a tear fest."

Oliver said and wiped a tear away.

"Let's get happy!"

Martin said.

Martin ordered another round of drinks, and he started telling some of his favorite jokes.

"A Rabbi, a Priest, and a Minister go into a bar, and one of them says..."

In another couple of minutes, we were laughing and having a great time. Oliver added some of his favorite jokes, and the drinks came for round two. Martin took me out on the dance floor, and we boogied to some disco.

"Oh man, I love that song, what happened to disco, it wasn't that bad!"

I told them.

"Even though Martin and I were just little kids when it was popular, I still love the music too!"

Oliver replied, waving his arms in the air and working on his third glass of wine.

"We should have a disco party, that would be fun!"

Martin suggested.

I took a drink and told them, "Ok, when Kendle's reopens, we are having a karaoke disco night every Wednesday in dedication to you guys cheering me up during the middle of the week.

"Oh girl, you are on, that sounds like fun!"

Oliver shouted.

"I'll have to go and buy a white suit." Martin laughed.

Just then, a very good-looking guy came by our table. He smiled at me and asked:

"Hi, I don't mean to interrupt, but would you like to dance?"

He asked me.

I looked at Martin and Oliver; they nodded in approval.

"Sure." I walked to the dance floor with him, and we started to dance. He was a good dancer, and we moved in sync.

The lights on the dance floor were green and pink strobes, and the disco ball glittered high above us.

After a few songs, we were tired, and I needed a drink, so I went back to my booth.

Martin and Oliver clapped for our great dance moves.

The good-looking dude then asked me, "How about dinner tomorrow night?"

Oh no, it was still too early for this; my heart was still raw, and I was done with this for now.

"Thanks, but I'm going to have to say no."

"Ok, well, have a nice evening."

He smiled; he was a gentleman.

"Thanks." I waved.

"Wow, he was really good-looking and so nice. What happened, Nikki?"

"Yeah, I know, but in my mind, I kept telling myself, remember the two guys who just dumped you."

Martin and Oliver looked at me sympathetically!

"Well, we at least have disco Wednesdays to look forward to, right?"

"Absolutely!" They said in unison.

We clinked our glasses and toasted to

DISCO.

Epilogue

Roxy and I stopped by Starbucks and ordered some lattes, a small breakfast, and a short conversation with Jessica.

"What color are you getting, Nikki?"

"I ordered one in red, and we're going to pick it up right after this. I'm so excited."

"I'm happy for you, wow! A new car!"

Jessica was giddy.

The day was sunny, 76 degrees, and a light breeze. I love California, my home, my state. Despite the downfalls, it will always be home!

Roxy and I arrived right on time,

At John Wayne's Jeep/Chrysler/Dodge of Rancho Niguel, the salesman asked me to be there at 10 am. Roxy pulled her 69' Camaro into the second visitor's parking stall, and we walked into the large showroom.

Vehicles were parked in the lobby, showcasing the most high-end and newest models of cars. There were Cherokees, Chargers, Challengers, Ram 2500s, Chrysler 300s, and a Jeep 4xe. All of them in many fabulous colors.

A saleswoman walked up to us, "How can I help you two ladies today?"

"I'm here to pick up my car. I'm working with Jazz Montgomery."

"Oh, cool, yeah, I'll get Jazz for you."

She walked off to get my salesman.

"Roxy, look at the Challengers, are they cool or what?"

"They're looking good; I might need to get one."

"We'll take your awesome 69 Camaro."

Jazz, the salesman, came up to us offering.

"Oh, no way, Cami stays with me forever, she's my baby, I was just maybe thinking of adding to my collection," Roxy replied.

"Aw shucks, well, I can definitely get you into a Challenger if you like."

"I'll think about it," Roxy replied.

He handed her his business card, "Let me know," and then turned to me.

"Now then, for Ms. Rodriguez, we have a Jeep here for you."

He smiled.

My Jeep pulled up in front of the showroom. "Looks like it just came out of being washed and waxed."

Jazz informed us.

We walked outside to my new Jeep, and a young dude hopped out of it and handed me a fob.

"Here you are, Ms. Rodriguez, it's ready to go."

"Thank you."

"Now, Ms. Rodriguez, you know how this works; it's a keyless start. Your fob can unlock and lock your doors. See, it has sensors to detect when the fob is on you. All you have to do is lift the door handle, and it opens. Then, with just a push of a button on your fob, you can lock the door. Plus, it's a push-button start, so just keep the fob close, and that about covers it. Do you have any questions for me?"

"No, I think you covered everything on our first visit. I'm ready to go."

"We appreciate your business, and as a thank you for purchasing a vehicle at John Wayne Jeep/Chrysler and Dodge, we have this for you."

He handed me a small basket with car wash soap, a microfiber towel, some air fresheners, a red coffee tumbler that read JEEP GIRL, and a small bottle of Armor All.

"Thank you, Jazz, it's wonderful."

We shook hands.

"You're welcome, and I can't wait for your band to play at Kendle's again. I'm a fan."

"Thanks, Jazz."

I climbed into my new red 4-door Jeep Wrangler Rubicon and hit the sky one-touch power top; it was basically like an extremely long sunroof or hybrid convertible. With the wind in my hair, I drove off.

Just then, Sam Chavez, my construction contractor, called me to go over some details of the rebuild on kendles.

"Nikki, we are getting started tomorrow, and everything is a green light on the building plans, and the permits have been approved."

"That's good news, Sam, thanks, I'll see you tomorrow."

I pulled into the parking lot of the Youth Center and walked in. I headed to my office to get some work done. Tito and Daisy followed me for temporary posts working at the Youth Center while Kendle's was under construction. I kept them on salary, and their contributions here have been well-received.

I offered Chef Stark a position here as well; he teaches a few culinary cooking classes for the youth, and I kept him on salary, too! Along with my loyal servers and Ken, my part-time bartender. They found positions here on a temp basis until we get Kendle's up and running, which, according to Sam, should just be two months.

"Hey, Boss," Tito called out.

"Good morning, are you heading to your wrestling class?"

"Sure am, the kids are going to learn some new moves today, they are doing fantastic. You know, if it's ok, I'd like to continue a class here, one or two a week when Kendle's is back up. Daisy and I love the kids."

"Absolutely, we need more instructors; I think it's a great idea."

"It won't interfere with our jobs at Kendle's; I promise, boss." Tito sold me.

"It sounds good; I like it."

He went off to his class, and I went into my office.

I set down my things and pulled out my MacBook from my black bag.

I was working for a few minutes when my phone rang, RNPD the screen read.

"Hello."

"Hi Nikki, this is Sonya. I've been assigned your case, and I have news about your nail gun attacker."

"Ok, what is it?"

"Your attacker is female."

I gasped, I knew it...

Don't miss the next exciting Nikki

Rodriguez adventure

Dates, Drugs, and Disco

Newly single Nikki Rodriguez isn't giving up on love yet,
even after Cupid's arrow shot her in the rear!

With her love life in the dumps, Nikki focuses on working at the
Youth Center and getting Kendle's Restaurant rebuilt. But Roxy
takes matters into her own hands and signs Nikki up for the new
and hot match-making service in town.

Sara gives Matt an earful about why Nikki kept her secret from
him, and Martin and Oliver help Matt plan a big Disco party for
Sara's 16th birthday. Things start to get hot in Rancho Niguel, and
Paul has his hands full when a body is found, and evidence points
to one of the bachelors of the match-making service.

With Stacie still pining for him and with the mayor pressuring for
an arrest, will he be able to protect Nikki from dating the bachelor
killer?

ABOUT THE AUTHOR

M.A.Hansen

From a young age, M.A. Hansen has been writing short stories, poems, and novels for fun. This series is her first set of independently published books.
Her hobbies include reading mysteries, hiking, crocheting, and an infinite love of cooking and baking.
M.A. spends her time in the PNW and in sunny Southern California with her wonderful husband of 30 years. She is a mother and now a grandmother.
"I hope you enjoy reading about the adventure with my character, Nikki Rodriguez, a journey of love, mystery, and laughs."
M.A. Hansen